DESPERATE RESCUE

VANISHING RANCH
BOOK 10

CHRISTY BARRITT

COMPLETE BOOK LIST

Squeaky Clean Mysteries:

  #1 Hazardous Duty

  #2 Suspicious Minds

  #2.5 It Came Upon a Midnight Crime (novella)

  #3 Organized Grime

  #4 Dirty Deeds

  #5 The Scum of All Fears

  #6 To Love, Honor and Perish

  #7 Mucky Streak

  #8 Foul Play

  #9 Broom & Gloom

  #10 Dust and Obey

  #11 Thrill Squeaker

  #11.5 Swept Away (novella)

  #12 Cunning Attractions

  #13 Cold Case: Clean Getaway

#14 Cold Case: Clean Sweep

#15 Cold Case: Clean Break

#16 Cleans to an End

While You Were Sweeping, A Riley Thomas Spinoff

The Sierra Files:

#1 Pounced

#2 Hunted

#3 Pranced

#4 Rattled

The Gabby St. Claire Diaries (a Tween Mystery series):

#1 The Curtain Call Caper

#2 The Disappearing Dog Dilemma

#3 The Bungled Bike Burglaries

The Worst Detective Ever

#1 Ready to Fumble

#2 Reign of Error

#3 Safety in Blunders

#4 Join the Flub

#5 Blooper Freak

#6 Flaw Abiding Citizen

#7 Gaffe Out Loud

#8 Joke and Dagger

#9 Wreck the Halls

#10 Glitch and Famous

#11 Not on My Botch

Raven Remington

Relentless

Holly Anna Paladin Mysteries:

#1 Random Acts of Murder

#2 Random Acts of Deceit

#2.5 Random Acts of Scrooge

#3 Random Acts of Malice

#4 Random Acts of Greed

#5 Random Acts of Fraud

#6 Random Acts of Outrage

#7 Random Acts of Iniquity

Lantern Beach Mysteries

#1 Hidden Currents

#2 Flood Watch

#3 Storm Surge

#4 Dangerous Waters

#5 Perilous Riptide

#6 Deadly Undertow

Lantern Beach Romantic Suspense

#1 Tides of Deception

Lantern Beach Blackout: The New Recruits

#1 Rocco

#2 Axel

#3 Beckett

#4 Gabe

Lantern Beach Mayday

#1 Run Aground

#2 Dead Reckoning

#3 Tipping Point

Lantern Beach Blackout: Danger Rising

#1 Brandon

#2 Dylan

#3 Maddox

#4 Titus

Lantern Beach Christmas

Silent Night

Crime á la Mode

#1 Dead Man's Float

#2 Milkshake Up

#3 Bomb Pop Threat

#4 Banana Split Personalities

Beach Bound Books and Beans Mysteries

#2 Breakwater Protector

#3 Cape Corral Keeper

#4 Seagrass Secrets

#5 Driftwood Danger

#6 Unwavering Security

Beach House Mysteries

#1 The Cottage on Ghost Lane

#2 The Inn on Hanging Hill

#3 The House on Dagger Point

School of Hard Rocks Mysteries

#1 The Treble with Murder

#2 Crime Strikes a Chord

#3 Tone Death

Carolina Moon Series

#1 Home Before Dark

#2 Gone By Dark

#3 Wait Until Dark

#4 Light the Dark

#5 Taken By Dark

Suburban Sleuth Mysteries:

Death of the Couch Potato's Wife

Fog Lake Suspense:

#1 Edge of Peril

#2 Margin of Error

#3 Brink of Danger

#4 Line of Duty

#5 Legacy of Lies

#6 Secrets of Shame

#7 Refuge of Redemption

Cape Thomas Series:

#1 Dubiosity

#2 Disillusioned

#3 Distorted

Standalone Romantic Mystery:

The Good Girl

Suspense:

Imperfect

The Wrecking

Sweet Christmas Novella:

Home to Chestnut Grove

Standalone Romantic-Suspense:

Keeping Guard

The Last Target

Race Against Time

Ricochet

Key Witness

Lifeline

High-Stakes Holiday Reunion

Desperate Measures

Hidden Agenda

Mountain Hideaway

Dark Harbor

Shadow of Suspicion

The Baby Assignment

The Cradle Conspiracy

Trained to Defend

Mountain Survival

Dangerous Mountain Rescue

Nonfiction:

Characters in the Kitchen

Changed: True Stories of Finding God through Christian Music (out of print)

The Novel in Me: The Beginner's Guide to Writing and Publishing a Novel (out of print)

CHAPTER
ONE

CHARLIE SOLDIER PRESSED her back against the brick of the stately house and let the chilly February wind sweep over her.

She glanced beside her at Detective Pierce Bradshaw. He gave her a nod.

Pierce was the last man she wanted to work with, but desperation had brought her back to him.

Together, they started toward the back of the dark, quiet house nestled on the dark, quiet street.

The house belonged to Frank and Shannon Turley. Alias: Ernest and Katherine Hollis.

The two had been hard-hitting reporters who'd won several awards for their in-depth investigative work. The retired journalists were both in their late sixties now but still wrote the occasional feature or editorial.

Charlie and Pierce had stationed themselves outside the house for the past hour. They'd seen no signs of life, other than a light most likely set on a timer that popped on at the front porch precisely at eight.

Were these two in the wind?

It was a good possibility. But Charlie needed to know for sure before she started chasing after something that might not exist.

The Turleys had the answers she urgently needed.

Or they could be involved with the criminal enterprise Charlie was trying to take down.

For that reason, she and Pierce had to be careful.

Pierce had already knocked at the door. There was no answer.

He'd tried to reach them by phone. Again, no answer.

But money had disappeared from the couple's bank account three days ago.

Charlie needed to know if the couple was holed up inside or if they'd run.

She and Pierce crept around the perimeter of the house toward the back. As she moved, she peeked into each window she passed.

No signs of life inside the house caught her eye.

Finally, once they'd circled the entire place,

Charlie and Pierce met in the shadows of the sycamore tree behind the house.

"What now?" Pierce stared at her with that intense gaze he was known for.

"We don't know what's happening upstairs."

"I hope you're not suggesting breaking and entering." He gave her a knowing look. "You want to get me fired?"

When Charlie had known him before, he'd been studying criminal justice with plans of going into the police academy. Now, fifteen years later, he was a lead homicide detective with the Baltimore PD. He still had that familiar arrogance about him—arrogance Charlie had once been attracted to.

"You don't have to do any of this with me." Charlie tugged the black knit hat covering her head. "I made that clear when I contacted you."

She hadn't wanted help per se. She'd mostly needed a contact in this area, someone who could do things she couldn't—like looking into the couple's finances.

Pierce's gaze remained sharp and unchanged. "It's not safe for you to do this alone."

She couldn't argue with him. She had plenty of guys on her payroll she could have brought with her. In fact, in normal circumstances, she would have sent someone else to do this job.

But this mission was personal. Charlie wanted these answers for herself.

Besides, most of her guys were busy right now with other assignments. So when Pierce had offered to lend her a hand . . . she'd figured it might be good to have a local cop nearby.

"I'm going in." Charlie nodded toward the back door. "Are you going to arrest me?"

Pierce gave her another look. "Only if someone catches us."

"Sounds fair." She pulled a kit from her pocket and began to pick the back door lock.

She felt Pierce's gaze on her as she worked.

"Where'd you learn that?" he finally asked. "You've developed some new skills since we were last together."

She didn't like the way he said, "last together."

She'd prefer to erase that period of her life.

"I'm always trying to improve myself." Charlie shrugged and kept working the lock mechanism. "What can I say?"

Pierce let out a soft chuckle. "That's what I've always loved about you. That sassy mouth, stubborn determination, and biting wit."

She let his words roll off her back. She'd learned long ago not to let the man get under her skin.

Finally, a click sounded.

Charlie shoved the kit back into her pocket and quietly opened the door.

As she stepped inside, she grabbed the gun holstered at her waist.

The stakes were high. She needed to be careful—just in case danger lurked nearby.

She had a lot of reasons to stay alive.

Her daughter, Amberly, being one of them.

Finding answers about her father was another.

And Monroe . . .

A knot lodged in her throat at the thought of him being in a coma in the hospital.

Her heart ached at the thought of all three. Tragedy surrounded each.

She still had the chance to make things right—and she was determined to do just that.

But she set those thoughts aside for now. She needed to stay focused on the mission at hand. She couldn't afford any mistakes.

Inside, Pierce nodded at her, and they split up to cover more ground.

Charlie went left and remained along the kitchen wall, listening for any signs of trouble as she moved. A rotten scent filled the air.

Trash that hadn't been taken out for weeks?

Maybe.

Maybe not.

They checked the downstairs first, and it was just as she thought.

No one was here.

But the bedrooms were upstairs, and it was ten at night.

The Turleys could be in bed.

Side by side, she and Pierce climbed the steps to the second floor.

Three bedrooms waited there and, if Charlie had to guess, the master bedroom would be on the right.

Yes, she'd studied the blueprint of the house before their covert operation this evening.

Any smart operative would.

It was hard to call herself an operative considering she ran the organization and called the shots. But that was exactly how she felt at the moment.

She was no longer the decision maker.

She was the boots on the ground.

She planted herself on one side of the bedroom door, and Pierce stood on the other.

With a nod to each other, Pierce nudged the door open.

Darkness stared back.

Along with the rotten odor she'd noticed earlier. It was stronger here—enough to make her want to throw up.

Nausea gurgled in her stomach as the truth teased her senses.

Pierce turned on his flashlight and scanned the room.

The beam stopped at the bed.

Two figures lay there.

"Hello?" he called.

Silence answered.

She and Pierce crept closer. The flashlight revealed a couple lying beneath the dark blue bedspread.

Pierce didn't call out again.

Instead, he paused by the bed and shined his light on the figures.

They still hadn't moved.

At all.

Charlie frowned as she crept closer, refusing to breathe through her nose.

Not with that putrid scent in the room.

Pierce moved the covers back.

Gunshot wounds pierced both chests, and blood stained their clothes and sheets.

It was just as Charlie feared.

The Turleys were dead.

———

Twenty minutes later, the Baltimore PD arrived at the scene.

Pierce had called in the discovery, explaining that he'd done a wellness check on the couple after no one had heard from them for several days.

No one questioned him.

Probably because Pierce wasn't the kind of guy people liked to question. He was confident—overly so. The look in his eyes dared anyone to defy him.

The police had allowed Charlie to remain on scene—but outside—during the investigation. Pierce had introduced her as an old colleague.

She supposed that was semi-true.

But all she really cared about right now was figuring out what happened to the Turleys. Who had done this to them? When? Why?

Several minutes later, Pierce stepped from the front porch, took her arm, and pulled her toward the sidewalk, away from any listening ears.

Charlie observed him a split second. His lean build. His sharp gaze. His dark, thick hair and brisk movements.

He was handsome. Back when Charlie had known him, many women had thought so. At one time, so had Charlie.

The two of them had thoroughly enjoyed the party scene together in their younger days—and

Pierce had enjoyed the money Charlie's dad had left behind for her after his death.

She'd quickly gotten over her fascination with Pierce. Then again, it had been more than a decade since she'd seen him. People could change.

She certainly had.

"Okay, enough skating around the truth." His gaze bore into hers. "What's going on?"

Charlie was surprised it had taken him so long to want more details. She'd been grateful he hadn't asked more questions when she first approached him about coming to Baltimore.

But she understood why he wanted to know more after finding the Turleys' bodies.

She glanced around, making sure no one was close.

Then she started. "The Turleys went by the aliases of Mr. and Mrs. Ernest Hollis. I discovered they'd opened a safe deposit box in Vegas under that name."

He squinted. "You do know you have to have a photo ID to do that."

She resisted a scowl at his patronizing tone. "Yes, of course, I realize that."

She may have resisted a scowl, but her voice hardened. She needed to keep a cool head and not grow irritated. But Pierce had always brought out that side of her.

He remained unbothered by her tone. "How did you discover that?"

"It's not important." Charlie glanced at the officers talking in a circle in the distance. "It's what was inside that safe deposit box that's important."

His eyes narrowed even more. "I take it that somehow you know what was inside of it."

"I do. It was . . ." She paused long enough to consider her words before finishing. "Let's say it was highly sensitive classified information and interviews."

"With whom?"

"A top-level political leader."

His hands went to his hips. "You can't tell me a name?"

"It's better if I don't right now."

He rubbed his jaw and drew in a long breath.

He *had* matured some since Charlie had last worked with him. The old Pierce would have demanded answers, not giving up until he had what he wanted.

"How long ago did you discover this information in the safe deposit box?" he asked instead.

"Eight days ago."

Realization rolled over his features. "So you think that someone else knew that this information had been discovered and they killed the Turleys to keep them quiet?"

Her jaw tightened. "That's exactly what I think. In fact, this information fell into the hands of the Geminis."

He flinched. "The cartel? I thought they'd disbanded."

"They tried to 'reinvent' themselves. One of the top items on their list of things to do was getting their hands on this information."

His eyes narrowed again. "But that doesn't fit what they stand for. They're about drugs and human trafficking."

"And power and money. It's all tied together. Where there's one, there are the others. You know that."

He didn't deny her words. "I don't like where this is going. Politics. The cartel. Classified information. How did you even get yourself involved in this, Charlie?"

"It's a long story."

He continued to study her without apology. "Don't you run a horse rescue?"

Charlie had shared that part of her life with him when she'd initially called to ask for help. "A lot of what's been happening has taken place near my ranch. That makes this relevant to me."

He twisted his head skeptically. "There's gotta be more to it than that."

"That's all I can say."

As he started to ask another question, her phone rang.

Charlie grabbed the device from her pocket and shoved it against her ear, thankful for the interruption. "Charlie here."

"Hello, Ms. Soldier. This is Dr. Gray in Phoenix. I'm calling to let you know that Monroe Davis just woke up."

CHAPTER
TWO

MONROE GROANED as he shifted in his hospital bed. His thoughts felt muddy, and the clarity he sought seemed more like a distant dream.

He vaguely recalled a doctor coming in a few hours ago and muttering something—something Monroe couldn't remember the details of right now.

As his vision cleared, he glanced around the room.

The place felt cold and sterile . . . and empty of anything but medical equipment.

His heart panged at the realization.

How long had he been here? What had happened? What city was he even in?

At that thought, the door flung open, and someone flew inside.

He blinked several times, wondering if he was dreaming.

But when Charlie Soldier's face appeared in front of him, Monroe knew he wasn't.

Relief washed through him.

He'd never been so happy to see her beautiful face.

She grabbed his hand as she stood at his side and stared at him, tears welling in her gaze. "Monroe . . . you're awake."

"I am. But it's quite the headache I have." Even as he spoke the words aloud, his head pulsed with an insistent throb.

"I'm happy you still have a head that can ache."

He raised an eyebrow. "It was that bad, huh?"

A frown pulled at the sides of her lips. "You don't remember?"

He shook his head, which only made it pound harder. Monroe squeezed his eyes shut as he tried to get his brain to stop spinning.

Finally, he said, "I don't."

"I asked the doctor to let me tell you what happened." Charlie squeezed his hand harder. "I'm so sorry, Monroe."

Slowly, more details came into focus. The IV in his arm. The monitors hooked up to his chest. The oxygen cannula in his nose.

"What happened?" His voice sounded throaty as he asked the question. His mouth felt dry. His lips were cracked.

He was thirsty, he realized. But too nauseous to want to do anything about it.

He stared at Charlie, watching as she tried to formulate a response.

The woman was hardly ever at a loss for words.

So whatever she had to say must be bad.

Despite his racing thoughts, Monroe gave her space to figure out what she needed to say.

Charlie Soldier was the most beautiful woman he'd ever known—inside and out.

He'd loved her for a long time.

He simply couldn't tell her. He couldn't risk ruining their friendship.

Instead, he stayed quiet, treasuring the close comradery they did share.

Charlie licked her lips again before saying, "Monroe . . . the Geminis showed up at the lodge with guns, and they grabbed Natalie and Joshua. You remember who Natalie and Joshua are, right?"

An image of the general contractor and her crewmember-turned-secret-ICE-agent filled Monroe's mind.

He didn't try to nod this time. "I do."

He vaguely remembered showing up at the lodge,

ready to help after he'd been alerted about a situation that had arisen.

That's when the ambush had occurred.

He stiffened as slices of his memory came back.

"As cartel members attempted to escape, one of the guys threw a grenade." Charlie's voice cracked. "You were the one closest to it, and you took the brunt of the explosion."

"A grenade?" Monroe's heart beat harder, and he started to sit up.

Were his limbs still intact?

Panic like he'd never known before filled him.

What exactly had happened to him when that grenade went off?

Charlie pressed her hand into his chest. "It's okay."

He exhaled and leaned back on the bed, waiting to hear what else she had to say as he fought the overwhelming anxiety.

"The blast threw you onto the ground, and you hit your head. They put you in an induced coma to control the swelling on your brain. You had to get some stitches and part of your calf has a mild burn."

"Is that all?" Was there something she wasn't telling him?

"Isn't that enough?" Charlie squeezed his hand

tighter. "The good news is that the doctor said you're going to be okay. You just need time to recover."

"So I didn't lose anything?" Monroe held his breath as he waited for her answer.

"Just about a week of your time."

Relief washed through him.

In all his years playing professional football, he never remembered feeling as banged up as he did right now—like his body *and* mind were broken and battered.

But he was alive. Intact.

He glanced at Charlie again and saw the tears rolling down her cheeks.

This whole thing had shaken her up, hadn't it?

Monroe wondered for the first time since they'd met if maybe—just maybe—Charlie shared his feelings also.

———

Charlie didn't normally let her emotions get the best of her. Yet she couldn't seem to get a grip on herself right now.

All she wanted was to cry—both tears of joy and tears of despair over what had happened.

She was so thankful Monroe was here and that he was okay.

He'd been touch-and-go there for a while.

Monroe tried to push himself up in bed again and groaned. He'd never been one to show weakness. To see him like this now . . .

She swallowed the knot that rose in her throat.

Charlie wanted more than anything to take this pain away from him. But she couldn't.

Instead, she rested her hand along his jaw. "If you need to move, I can call a nurse to help. Don't hurt yourself."

Monroe waved her off, but his face remained distorted with discomfort. "I'm fine."

The way his jaw hardened as he said the words told the truth of the matter.

He was still in a lot of pain.

Charlie studied his face a moment. The former linebacker had a muscular, burly build and strong features. His eyes were crystal blue, but his gaze was hooded. His brown hair was hassle-free with his short—almost completely shaven—cut. He towered a good foot above her, his thick chest acting as her shield whenever trouble came close.

Now trouble had nearly gotten him killed.

More guilt filled Charlie. He wouldn't have been in harm's way if not for her.

"What happened after the Geminis showed up?"

His voice sounded hoarse as he asked the question, his gaze locking on hers. "Where are Natalie and Joshua? Are they okay?"

"Natalie and Joshua managed to get away from the cartel. We got Bella back also." Bella was Joshua's cousin who'd been abducted by the cartel. The situation had been ugly—but everything had worked out in the end.

Everything except Monroe.

Monroe's shoulders seemed to soften. "That's good news, at least."

"It *is* good news."

"What's going on?" His head dropped back onto his pillow as if he were settling in for a long conversation. "What have I missed the past week?"

Charlie gently stroked her thumb along his cheek. "Why don't you just worry about your recovery first? We'll worry about the rest later."

His hand covered hers, pressing it against his neck and jaw. "You don't have to tiptoe around me. I'm going to be fine."

Charlie swallowed hard and pulled herself together. "Of *course* you're going to be fine."

But she hadn't believed that to be true when she'd first seen him covered in blood after the explosion. Or when she'd watched the medical helicopter airlift him off the ranch and take him away. If she had, she wouldn't feel this emotional right now.

Charlie hadn't spoken the words aloud, but she'd feared Monroe wouldn't come out of his coma. Or, if he did, that he'd never be the same. Head trauma could change people . . .

And it would be her fault.

Charlie cleared her throat, trying to hold back those thoughts and emotions. "After the cartel abducted Natalie and Joshua, they forced them undercover, disguised as a couple named Ernest and Katherine Hollis. They had to retrieve items from a safe deposit box at a bank in Vegas."

"What was so special about this box?" Monroe narrowed his eyes, surprisingly sharp and alert considering his condition.

"Inside were pictures of former President Bill Radar from approximately fifteen years ago. Based on the images, it appears he was doing some back-room deals with some unscrupulous people."

Monroe's eyes narrowed. "Like who?"

"Business owners—both from the US and abroad. Entertainment leaders—like the head honcho of a major motion picture company. Financial geniuses. Most of them are people whose faces you wouldn't recognize. But when you figure out who they are, you realize that they're powerful."

"Is that all they found inside the box?"

"There were also cassette tape recordings of Radar speaking to someone. The Overland Hotel was mentioned."

Monroe squeezed her hand tighter and sucked in a breath. "The hotel where your grandmother died in the so-called terrorist bombing . . ."

"Exactly."

His gaze locked with hers. "This is big, Charlie."

"I know."

"So who are these people? The Hollises?"

"They were journalists. Their real names were Frank and Shannon Turley."

Monroe's eyes widened. "What do you mean *were*?"

"I just went to pay them a visit but . . ." Charlie licked her lips as she tried to choose her words. "Someone else got to them first."

"How did they die?"

"They were shot point-blank in the chest while they slept. Police in Maryland are working the case, and I have a contact there who said he'll keep me informed."

"This could be the lead that you've been looking for, the clue that will tell you what exactly happened at that hotel and who really killed your father."

"I know." But again, the words nearly stuck in Charlie's throat.

She'd been working for the past two years to learn what really happened. Someone who'd served in her father's Army squad had contacted her and said there was more to her dad's death than the government had reported. They'd said he died in hostile fire.

Charlie had discovered there *was* more to the story. In fact, it seemed as if someone in the Army had killed her father and made it look like foreign enemies were responsible.

The man who'd given her that information had also mysteriously died before they could meet in person and talk.

But as Charlie had researched more, she'd discovered another squad member had found information indicating the terrorist attack that had killed her grandmother—and ultimately motivated her father to join the military—may not have been the work of international terrorists as the media had reported.

Charlie had dug into the theory and uncovered information indicating that the whole hotel bombing may have been a cover-up for something else, something domestic.

Now she felt so close to finding answers.

But her first priority was to make sure Monroe recovered.

Because her life would never be the same if he didn't. When she imagined her future without Monroe at her side, everything seemed so bleak.

That was a reality she couldn't face.

CHAPTER
THREE

CHARLIE SPENT the next three days at the hospital with Monroe.

It had been a grueling time for him, but Dr. Gray said Monroe was recovering well. He'd probably have to stay in the hospital another week, but it didn't appear he had any long-term damage from the blast.

Now, as Monroe slept in the bed, Charlie sat beside him and squeezed his hand. Some of the medicine they'd given him had knocked him out.

He was usually so strong, and she wasn't used to seeing him like this. The sight of it left her feeling unnerved.

For the past three years, Monroe had always been her rock, the person she could depend on.

But they were friends—and only friends. Charlie

had vowed to remain single and independent until the day she died. Every time she'd given a relationship a chance, the results had been abysmal.

Besides, being single allowed her to focus all her efforts on her life mission: to help those who were helpless.

Relationships . . . well, they took time to nurture and grow.

But nothing felt the same when Monroe wasn't by her side.

Charlie sighed and leaned back, adjusting the papers in her lap.

She'd brought her laptop with her and tried to work when either Monroe was sleeping or when she had to leave the room to give him privacy.

She was still waiting to hear an update from Pierce. The only thing he'd told her so far was that the Turleys had died from gunshot wounds to their chest—a fact she'd seen firsthand. The medical examiner estimated they'd been dead four days before their bodies were discovered.

And the money taken from their accounts?

They'd taken it out themselves. Charlie could only assume they'd felt threatened and had been about to run. Someone had gotten to them first.

However, the person behind the crime still remained a mystery.

Not only that, but everyone the police had spoken with claimed the couple was nice, not the type to have enemies.

Security cameras on nearby houses hadn't picked up on any unusual neighborhood visitors, no unidentified fingerprints had been left inside their house, and no trace evidence offered any leads.

But Charlie hadn't come this far to reach a dead end.

Since the couple had used an alias at the bank, figuring out who they really were had been a challenge. Their safe deposit box had to be accessed via a biometric fingerprint scan, which meant their prints were on file at the bank.

Charlie had pulled multiple strings to get a copy of those prints—she'd called in a lot of favors—but she'd finally obtained them.

Eventually, with the help of her team, she'd matched the prints to the Turleys.

She had eventually located the couple in Baltimore.

She'd wanted to talk to them in person.

Had almost had the answers she needed . . . but she'd been too late.

Charlie's phone rang.

She pulled it from her purse, and her heart

skipped a beat when she saw Pierce's name on her screen.

Maybe he finally had an update.

She shoved the phone to her ear. "Hello?"

"Charlie," Pierce said. "I think we might have finally tracked down a lead."

She shifted. "Well, don't keep me in suspense."

"I contacted an editor the Turleys used to work with—someone who's willing to talk to me. Says she knows something."

Charlie's heart quickened. "Is that right?"

"Unfortunately, she has lung cancer and isn't doing well. With the Turleys dead and with this woman being on death's doorstep, she's ready to talk. From the sounds of it, she's been waiting for someone to ask her the right questions. Do you want to go with me to meet with her?"

Charlie's heart pumped harder. "I'd love to. When do I need to be there?"

She glanced at Monroe as she felt the warring obligations inside her.

"Unfortunately, tonight. Do you think you can get here in time?"

She glanced at the clock. It was one o'clock now. She was in Phoenix, and Pierce was in Baltimore.

Thankfully, that shouldn't hold her back.

"I'll be there," she told him.

As she ended the call, Charlie glanced at Monroe again as he slept, his chest evenly rising and falling. The cannula in his nose was gone, but he still had his IV and several monitors. Hopefully, they would be removed soon.

She was ready to get him back home—but only once doctors said it was safe to do so.

She leaned closer, planting a soft kiss on his cheek before whispering, "I'll be back soon."

Charlie knew Monroe would understand why she needed to leave.

Yet her heart still felt as if it were torn in two.

———

When Monroe had awoken several hours ago, the nurse had given him a message from Charlie: she had to go but promised to check in soon.

He understood. Something had come up that she needed to deal with. It came with the territory.

But he missed her terribly.

Something about being in the hospital alone . . . it made him reevaluate his future. Made him think about his singleness. About how growing old alone had never been in his plans.

He frowned and pushed down the thoughts.

Dwelling on things that were out of his control wouldn't help his recovery.

Or was the future something he *could*—to an extent—control? Maybe there were changes he needed to make as soon as he blew this joint.

But what would those changes look like? Change almost always came with pain.

Was he willing to go there?

Again, he pushed the thoughts down. He needed to think about that more later.

Even though the doctor had said Monroe would be here another week, Monroe had decided it would be four—maybe five—days max.

He wanted to get back to the ranch. To oversee things there. To regain his life.

Yet he was grateful to still be alive. Things could be very different right now. He could have lost a limb when that grenade exploded.

Or he could've lost his life.

He pushed himself higher up on the bed, knowing it was almost time for physical therapy.

A knock sounded at the door, and he looked up.

A woman in blue scrubs stepped into the room and flashed a smile. He'd never seen her before, but that wasn't unusual here at the hospital. There seemed to be an endless stream of staff coming in and out on different shifts.

"Good afternoon, Mr. Davis. I'm Nurse Mary. How are you feeling?" The brunette with the pixie haircut paused near the foot of his bed.

"Been better. Been worse."

She chuckled softly. "I can understand that feeling. The doctor ordered a dose of this new medication for you before I take you down for a CT scan."

"Dr. Gray didn't tell me anything about a new medication. What's it for? And why do I need another CT scan? I just had one yesterday." The doctor already said nothing was broken and that the shrapnel hadn't hit any major arteries.

Nurse Mary smiled. "That's a lot of questions. You know I'm just following orders, right? Dr. Gray isn't the only doctor on staff here."

Monroe didn't crack a smile. "Which doctor ordered the CT scan?"

The nurse looked at the electronic pad in her hands. "Looks like it was . . . Dr. Walters."

He didn't recognize the name. "Again, what do I need another CT scan for?"

She placed her tablet on the edge of his bed and paced closer to check his vitals instead. "Like I said, I don't ask questions. I just do what I'm told. I can have the doctor come in if you'd like, but that will probably only delay your release from the hospital. Dr. Walters has already left for the day and won't be back to do his rounds until tomorrow morning."

"I don't want a CT scan, not until I know exactly what it's for. The bills really rack up, you know."

But it wasn't about money for Monroe.

Maybe his brain was still scarred from the trauma his body had been through.

However, something about this conversation felt off.

Nurse Mary reached into the pocket of her scrub apron and pulled out a syringe. She started to reach for his IV. "You might feel a little sting as this goes into your IV—"

His instincts shot on high alert, and he jerked his hand away from her. "What's in that syringe?"

Her pleasant expression turned terse—but just for a split second. "Just something I need to give you before the CT scan to help you relax."

Had this woman already forgotten that he'd said no? "I want to talk to the doctor first, even if that means I'm in here longer."

When he looked at her again, something in her gaze changed.

Gone was the personable nurse.

In her place was someone calculated and twisted —and someone who didn't want to be deterred.

CHAPTER
FOUR

CHARLIE ARRIVED in Baltimore in time for the meeting.

On the flight, she'd made several calls—including more than one to the ranch so she could check on things there. Amberly, her teenage daughter, was being privately tutored. Her teacher hadn't given Charlie a good report, however.

That meant Charlie and Amberly were going to have to have another long talk when she got back.

They'd had many of those.

As soon as she was cleared to exit the plane, she hurried down the steps toward Pierce's waiting SUV.

Together, they took off to meet Margaret Creighton.

In between phone calls about Amberly, Charlie

had researched Margaret Creighton during the four-hour flight.

The woman appeared to be someone you didn't mess with.

Now nearly seventy years old, Margaret had been senior editor for the *Washington Ledger* for twenty years until she retired four years ago.

She had a reputation for being both exacting and demanding. When reporters made a mistake, they were fired—because there was no room for mistakes in journalism, Margaret had been quoted. As a result, the woman had developed a reputation for her reliability, attention to detail, and the ability to remain unbiased.

"I can't wait to hear what she has to say," Charlie glanced at Pierce. "Thanks for including me on this."

"I can't believe you got here in time," Pierce said as they headed down the road.

"This isn't the first time I've had to travel at the last minute." Thankfully, Charlie had a pilot on standby, a man named Nate "Ghost" Casper, who was always reliable and trustworthy.

An hour after she'd called Ghost, he'd landed at a private airport, and they'd been on their way not long after.

A few minutes later, she and Pierce pulled up to a

historic-looking home. The place was big and stately, surrounded by other homes of equal stature.

From what Charlie had read, Margaret's husband had worked for Wall Street. That explained how an editor could afford a place like this.

Pierce knocked at her door, and a woman in pink scrubs answered and introduced herself as Nancy, the home health nurse. She led them upstairs to Margaret's room.

The place was dark with the shades drawn and a small bedside light casting barely any illumination. A scent Charlie couldn't quite identify—but it reminded her of a nursing home—along with a faint scent of lavender, filled the room.

A woman lay in a hospital bed, blanket tucked around her. Her face—once vibrant and youthful—now appeared pale and bony.

She didn't have much time left, did she?

Compassion swelled in Charlie at the thought.

Pierce stepped toward the bed. "Mrs. Creighton . . . I'm Detective Pierce Bradshaw with the Baltimore Police Department. This is a colleague of mine, Charlie Soldier."

As he mentioned her name, Margaret's eyes glimmered. She looked Charlie over before nodding. "I know who you are."

Charlie was used to that reaction. Her father had

been an icon to so many people—almost a legend after his death. He'd won three Super Bowls before giving up his football career.

"Thank you for letting me come," Charlie said.

"Of course." Margaret coughed, the sound continuing for several minutes.

Charlie handed her the glass of water tucked amongst the pill bottles on her nightstand.

Margaret took a few small sips before handing the glass back.

Charlie knew by looking at the woman that she was nervous. Her arms trembled ever so slightly, and her breathing was too shallow. Despite that, Margaret put on a strong front. Her voice sounded steady, and her gaze didn't break.

That was courage.

"I understand you used to work with the Turleys," Pierce started.

Margaret nodded and leaned back. "That's right. They were both excellent reporters and never let anyone intimidate them. They followed their instincts, which were extraordinary. Their deaths are a huge loss to the journalism community."

"Do you have any idea why someone may have killed them?" Charlie kept her voice soft but firm as she asked the question.

She didn't miss the brief exhale that escaped Margaret.

"I've kept quiet about this for years," her voice sounded weaker as she answered.

"How many years?" Charlie asked.

Margaret's gaze narrowed. "More than fifteen."

Charlie's heartbeat turned into a throb.

Fifteen years ago her grandmother had died in the Overland Hotel bombing.

All of Charlie's instincts told her Margaret was just the person she needed to talk to.

She couldn't wait to ask more questions.

But, before she could, Margaret continued, "You're going to want to sit down for this . . ."

———

Monroe held his arm up as he saw Nurse Mary come at him with a syringe filled with some type of amber liquid.

The look in her eyes had turned to pure evil.

This woman wasn't a nurse.

She was a trained operative.

Someone had hired her to kill him, hadn't they?

Monroe might be weak from his injuries, but there was no way he'd sit back and let this happen.

He caught the woman's wrist and twisted it.

She let out a grunt as she jerked around until Monroe had no choice but to release his grip on her arm.

Then she turned and, without missing a beat, lunged at him again.

He slammed his hand on the nurse-call button.

He didn't want any of the nurses to get hurt. Still, if someone else was in the room, maybe this woman would leave.

But the hospital staff were notoriously slow at getting to the room.

As Nurse Mary lunged at him with the syringe again, he blocked her with his arm.

The IV tore from the back of his hand, and blood began to stream onto his hospital gown.

He'd worry about that later.

"Who are you?" he grumbled as he caught the woman in a headlock.

"That's not important," she said through clenched teeth.

"It is to me."

"You should've backed off." Nurse Mary continued to struggle, her legs kicking but not reaching him.

"Backed off from what?" He held her more tightly.

"I think you and I both know the answer to that question."

As she said the words, she grabbed a fork left over from his lunch tray and jammed it into his leg.

Monroe let out a growl.

The woman seized the opportunity and darted back to her feet.

She grabbed the syringe that had fallen onto the floor and dove toward him again.

Monroe rolled out of the way and off the bed, crashing to the floor.

His shoulder throbbed upon impact. Pain reverberated through his multiple injuries. Equipment clattered around him.

He looked up in time to see the needle plunge into the mattress where he'd been sitting seconds before.

Footsteps hurried down the hall. Help was coming.

"This isn't over." The woman sneered at him as she rose to her feet. "I'll be back."

She sprinted from the room just before medical staff flooded inside.

"FRANK AND SHANNON called me one day about fifteen years ago," Margaret started. "They were excited. Said they got a lead on a story that would make them the next Woodward and Bernstein."

"Did they tell you what this story was about?" Charlie could hardly breathe as she waited for the answer. So much hinged on what Margaret said.

"Not at that time, no. They said they needed more evidence first. But they were so excited they wanted me to know something big was coming. I didn't hear from them for a couple of months, and I figured their idea didn't pan out."

"And then?" Pierce crossed his arms as he listened.

"Then they called again and told me that they

believed the bombing of the Overland Hotel wasn't the work of terrorists, that it was domestic."

Charlie's heart beat harder.

"What?" Pierce muttered.

Not many people had heard the theory. But Charlie had more than once recently, so it didn't come as a surprise to her.

"They had a witness who was willing to go on record about it," Margaret said.

Charlie sucked in a breath at the revelation.

"If not terrorists, then who?" Pierce demanded.

"Have you heard of Jeffery Epstein?"

"Jeffery Epstein was behind this?" An incredulous tone filled Pierce's voice.

"No, but the story is similar. People in positions of power and influence were caught up in human trafficking and drug schemes. All of them thought they were untouchable."

"Then why the bombing?" Even though Charlie had her own theories, she didn't want Pierce to know she was already privy to some of these details.

"There were people at the hotel who knew too much. Besides, a war with a foreign country that the US had tense relations with would bury anyone's interest in this scheme. Collectively, the people behind this bombing had the connections and power to pull everything off. That's what the Turleys believed."

"Why haven't I heard about this?" Pierce demanded, his gaze hardening.

Margaret frowned. "Because the story was never published. One day, out of the blue, the Turleys came to me and told me the story didn't pan out and they were dropping it."

"What about the witness?" A touch of outrage filled Pierce's voice.

"The witness recanted her story. Without her, they didn't feel they had enough evidence to go public. Shannon told me they'd simply been sent on a wild goose chase."

"Did you believe her?" Charlie asked.

"I didn't have much choice. They didn't want to talk about it after that. It was all very strange."

Charlie knew the truth.

The Turleys had been intimidated.

But they *had* taken some of the information they discovered and had hidden it in that safe deposit box. The problem was someone else had learned it was there.

This person had most likely hired the cartel to retrieve the contents, knowing it would be too risky to get the information themselves.

But exactly who was calling the shots?

And why had the Turleys been killed now, all these years later?

Just then, Charlie's phone rang, and she saw the Phoenix area code.

Her heart quickened.

She wanted to keep listening to Margaret.

But if someone was calling from the hospital, she didn't want to miss it.

Monroe wasn't usually the type who'd call just to chat. So if it happened to be him, then he was calling for a good reason. Plus, he didn't have his cell phone with him. It had been destroyed in the blast.

"Please, excuse me for a minute." Charlie stepped toward the door, not missing the questioning glance Pierce gave her.

They were at the crux of the conversation, and it was a terrible time to leave. But she had to answer.

She stepped into the hallway and gently closed the door as she answered. "This is Charlie."

"Charlie Soldier? This is Dr. Gray from Phoenix Medical. I'm afraid we had a situation here with Mr. Davis."

Her heart skipped a beat. A *situation*? "What kind of situation?"

"We had a breach of security. A woman claimed to be on staff here and tried to inject Mr. Davis with something. There was a struggle."

Charlie's lungs tightened until she could hardly breathe. "Is Monroe okay?"

"Overall, he's fine. But we're monitoring him as a precaution. He wanted us to call you to let you know what happened."

"Why didn't he call me? I want to talk to him, to hear his voice."

"I'm afraid he's down getting an MRI on his shoulder right now. During the struggle, he took a hard fall. We sent a local police officer with him, just in case this woman comes back."

Charlie pressed her eyes shut. "The woman got away?"

"Unfortunately, she did."

Her back muscles tightened.

She should have stayed with Monroe. If she had, maybe this wouldn't have happened.

"Tell him to hold on," Charlie murmured. "I'll be there as quickly as I can."

Had someone connected with either her grandmother's or dad's deaths caught wind she and Monroe were getting closer to answers? Had they gone after Monroe, knowing any harm done to him could derail Charlie?

She wasn't sure.

As soon as she ended that call, she dialed the number of one of her operatives, former FBI agent

Jesse Marx. He answered right away, and Charlie explained the situation to him.

"I'm glad Monroe is okay," Jesse said. "I never imagined he would be a target."

"Me either. I need you to go to the hospital. Take Hudson with you. Stand guard at that hospital room, and don't let anyone get inside without checking their credentials first. Do you understand?"

"Yes, ma'am."

"I want you there ASAP." She knew Ghost was still in Maryland with her, waiting to fly her back or she'd send the helicopter for Jesse.

However, Jesse and Hudson were smart. They'd figure out a way to get there quickly. In the meantime, the hospital staff were supposed to be keeping an eye on Monroe's door. They'd assured her the local police were also involved.

She didn't think anyone would be foolish enough to strike again. Not that quickly, at least.

She hated to cut this conversation with Margaret short, but all she could think about was seeing Monroe again—so she could confirm with her own eyes that he was truly okay.

She slipped her phone into her pocket and stepped back into the room.

As she did, the lamp on Margaret's nightstand went dark.

Shadows engulfed the room.

Charlie's breath caught.

Had the bulb burned out?

Or was something else going on here?

She flipped the light switch on the wall to make sure.

The electricity had gone out, she realized.

Everything in the house suddenly seemed eerie and silent.

What sense did that make? It wasn't even storming outside.

"Is everything okay?" Margaret's voice sounded shaky.

"Most likely." Charlie wanted to reassure the woman, even though a bad feeling brewed in her gut.

Pierce paced toward the window and pulled the curtain aside. "The neighbor's lights are on."

Someone knew Charlie and Pierce were talking to Margaret right now, didn't they?

They were coming to make sure the woman didn't share any secrets.

What would these people do next?

How could she and Pierce protect Margaret, Nancy, and themselves at the same time?

———

As Pierce's flashlight appeared on the other side of the room, the two of them exchanged a shadowed glance.

They needed to check this out.

But first, Pierce grabbed his phone and called in backup.

"What's going on?" Margaret's voice trembled even more as she asked the question.

"It's probably nothing," Charlie tried to reassure her again. "But we should check it out, just to be safe."

"What about Nancy? She's downstairs in the kitchen whipping up something for dinner."

Charlie and Pierce exchanged another glance.

They both feared something had happened to the woman.

"I'll go downstairs." Pierce withdrew his gun, and his voice hardened. "Charlie, you stay outside her door and make sure no one comes in."

Charlie nodded and pulled out her own gun. She never left home without it.

As Pierce stepped out, Charlie squeezed Margaret's hand one more time as she sensed the woman's rising apprehension. "I'm going to stand in the hallway. If I lock the door, can you unlock it when we need to get in?"

"There's a key above the door frame if I can't."

"Okay." Charlie patted her skeletal hand. "I'm going to be right outside your door."

"Be careful."

With one last squeeze, Charlie stepped into the hallway and quietly turned the lock before closing the door behind her.

The two-story house with its dark walls and trim stared back at her mockingly, almost as if teasing that it knew something she didn't.

Remaining near Margaret's door, Charlie paced toward the railing and glanced down at the first floor.

Where was Pierce? Why didn't she hear anything? And what about Nancy?

The questions continued to circle in her mind.

After double-checking Margaret's door once more to make sure it was locked, Charlie strode down the hallway. She needed to make sure no one lurked in one of the other rooms.

Probably eight doors lined the second story.

An old house like this with all its nooks and crannies made for a good game of hide-and-seek. But whoever was here wasn't here to play games.

Charlie's breath caught as she spotted a shadow moving up the stairs.

She raised her gun, ready to act.

The flashlight beam atop her pistol illuminated

the approaching figure, and Charlie's shoulders slumped.

"It's me." Pierce paused beside her and pushed the barrel of her gun away from him. "Someone knocked Nancy out. She's still breathing, though."

Charlie's heart beat harder. "That means someone's in the house . . ."

"I didn't see anyone downstairs, but they're here somewhere."

"What should we do?"

"You take the east side of the hallway, and I'll take the west," Pierce said. "Okay?"

Charlie nodded "I locked the door to Margaret's room. Someone's going to have to get through that first if they want to get to her. She should be okay."

"Let's make sure no one comes anywhere near her door."

Charlie started down the hallway, passing Margaret's room. She was careful with each and every step, not wanting to make any unnecessary noises.

She reached the doorway adjacent to Margaret's room and nudged it with her foot.

It wasn't latched.

Charlie slowly pushed it open.

More darkness waited for her inside.

Her eyes hadn't yet fully adjusted, and the drawn shades kept any light from filtering in.

She gripped her gun as she stepped into the room.

Her flashlight beam illuminated the guest bedroom in front of her.

Nothing looked disturbed, but Charlie would need to check the place out further to be sure.

As she took another step, a shadowy figure rushed her and tackled her to the floor.

CHAPTER
SIX

CHARLIE'S HIP hit the edge of the nightstand, and the lamp atop it clattered to the floor.

Before she could right herself, something hard slammed into the side of her face and knocked her down.

Stars flashed in her eyes as pain pulsed through her head.

She started to aim her gun, but it was gone.

She must have dropped it when the man pushed her to the floor.

She blinked and tried to make out his features. But he wore all black—including a ski mask. And he said nothing.

Charlie struggled to pull herself to her feet.

But before she could, the intruder smashed something else into the side of her head.

A fist? An object? She didn't know.

But her head throbbed with pain.

She let out a moan before muttering, "That was a bad idea."

Charlie raised her legs and kicked the man away from her.

He stumbled back.

"Hold it right there!" Pierce burst into the room, and his flashlight illuminated the intruder.

The man remained frozen for a split second before sprinting toward the window.

Pierce pulled the trigger, and a bullet sliced the air.

Glass shattered.

Charlie wasn't sure if the bullet hit the man *and* the window or only the window.

Either way, the man dove from the jagged second-story opening.

She gasped as she heard a loud thump outside.

Quickly, she pushed herself to her feet and followed behind Pierce as he darted toward the window.

As they glanced outside, they saw the man lying on the concrete sidewalk near two outdoor trash bins. His body contorted in an unnatural way.

An unnatural way that made it clear that he was . . . dead.

As Pierce rushed outside to make sure the man truly was dead, Charlie went into Margaret's room to check on her.

The woman's face looked even more ashen now.

"Mrs. Creighton." Charlie leaned in front of her as concern pulsed through her. "Are you okay? I know that was scary. But the man is gone now, and Nancy is fine."

Margaret only stared straight ahead as if in shock.

Charlie rubbed the woman's arms, trying to calm her. "It's over. You're safe."

But Margaret still didn't speak or move.

Charlie put a finger to her neck.

Her pulse was still present, but it was faint.

This whole event may have sent her into some kind of cardiac emergency.

"Help is on the way," Charlie murmured, feeling a well of anxiety rising in her.

Had this incident literally scared the woman to death?

Ambulances wailed in the distance.

Charlie prayed they got here in time.

"I . . ." Margaret opened her mouth and tried to talk but sputtered.

Charlie leaned closer. "You what?"

"I . . ." Margaret moved her lips, but no words came out.

Was she trying to make a last-minute request?

"What is it, Mrs. Creighton?"

"Lothario . . ."

"Lothario?" Charlie repeated, her forehead wrinkling. "Who is Lothario?"

Margaret stared at her, her eyes going still.

Charlie put a hand on her shoulder. "Mrs. Creighton, stick with us."

Still no movement.

She checked the woman's pulse again.

She held her breath as she waited to feel a heartbeat.

Wait . . . there it was.

Barely there. But she was still alive.

For now.

Just then, paramedics rushed inside and surrounded the dying woman.

Charlie stepped back to let them work.

Lothario?

Had she heard Mrs. Creighton correctly?

If so, who was this guy, and why had Margaret said his name?

CHARLIE HAD WAITED outside as police and paramedics took over the scene.

The intruder who'd jumped from the window was dead—from the fall. Pierce hadn't shot him.

The man had no identification on him. But police were currently searching for any out-of-place cars on the nearby streets that might help them to identify this guy.

Charlie suspected they wouldn't have any luck on their venture.

Meanwhile, paramedics had taken Mrs. Creighton to the hospital. It was as Charlie suspected—she'd gone into cardiac arrest. Charlie prayed she would recover.

They'd also treated Nancy. She'd been hit over the head but otherwise appeared to be okay.

At Pierce's insistence, paramedics had checked Charlie out. She would have a terrible bruise beside her eye, but she'd be fine.

However, she'd be lying if she said that whole incident hadn't shaken her up.

Wallace Masterson had taught her everything she knew about defending herself.

He'd been one of her father's mentors, a former football player turned FBI agent turned Head of Homeland Security. Wallace and his wife, Greta, had taken Charlie in when things turned tough for her after her father's death.

Though the older couple had passed away several years ago, Charlie wouldn't be the person she was today without them.

Finally, Pierce exited the house and paced toward her. "Are you sure you're okay?"

Charlie nodded, still reeling as she remembered the man lunging from the shadows and catching her by surprise. "I suppose. That man . . . he was strong."

"Do you have any idea who he was?"

"My guess is that he was hired. Or maybe someone had some dirt on him, something he'd rather die over than being caught and arrested." A professional would have fought harder instead of jumping to his death.

"Before the power went off, you said you had to

leave. Is everything okay?" Pierce stared at her with that intense gaze.

Monroe's attack flashed in Charlie's mind.

It had probably been an hour since that call, and she needed to get back to Arizona. Even though she trusted her guys, there were some things that were best handled herself.

"Thanks for the reminder," she said. "If you'll excuse me a minute, I need to follow up on that."

"Of course."

As she paced away, another officer stepped forward to speak with Pierce.

She knew standing on the side of the lawn was about as much privacy as she'd get in the situation right now.

She dialed Jesse's number, and he answered on the first ring.

"Are you in Phoenix yet?" she asked.

"We just got here about ten minutes ago. Ghost called a friend for us, and he picked us up and brought us here."

A small measure of relief filled her. "So you've had eyes on Monroe then?"

"He seems fine. More irritated than anything else."

Charlie fought a smile. That sounded like Monroe.

"Let him know I'll be there as soon as I can," she said. "I had something pop up here, and I can't leave quite yet."

"Everything okay?"

"I'll explain when I get there. Just hold the fort down in the meantime, okay?"

"You got it."

She slipped her phone back into her pocket. As she squinted, the side of her face throbbed. She'd need to put some ice on her bruises before they swelled more.

Pierce—who'd since finished his conversation with the other officers—strode toward her again. His hands were on his hips and his eyes narrowed.

Charlie knew what was coming.

"So, who is this Monroe guy?" he asked.

Apparently, he'd overheard part of Charlie's conversation. Why wasn't she surprised?

"A colleague," she answered.

"Just a colleague?"

The question felt personal—and Charlie didn't feel any obligation to get personal with Pierce. "He's a colleague who happens to be in the hospital and someone I feel responsible for."

Pierce tilted his head. "I'm reading more into it than that. Your tone and body language changed when his name was mentioned."

She didn't offer any more information. It wasn't any of his business.

"I'll need to leave here as soon as I can," she said. "There's a situation that happened with him that I can't ignore."

He stared at her a moment before nodding toward the street. "Go."

Charlie's eyebrows shot up. "You don't need me to stay?"

He shook his head. "I can have one of my guys drive you to the airport. I assume you'll be back? Maybe Margaret will be okay and will be able to tell us more."

"Maybe." But Charlie didn't feel that confident. "Thank you for including me today."

"I wish you could've gotten more of those answers you're looking for."

"I do too." With one last look at Margaret's house, Charlie stepped away.

She wanted to get back to Monroe in Phoenix.

She still hadn't told Monroe everything.

She wasn't exactly sure when she'd have that opportunity.

The more time that passed, the more Charlie felt convinced she needed to tell him—before something else stopped her.

She just had to rip off the Band-Aid and get it over with.

———

Monroe heard a knock at his door and darted up in bed.

Warmth filled him when he saw Charlie step inside his room.

But the warmth quickly disappeared when she pulled off her sunglasses and he saw her black eye.

A growl started from deep within him as his muscles bristled. "What happened?"

She paused by his bed and flippantly waved her hand as if it wasn't a big deal. "I'm fine."

He didn't believe her. "What happened?"

"I'll have plenty of time to fill you in later. Right now, I'm more concerned about you." Charlie squeezed his hand as she studied his face. "I can't believe what happened to you."

He shrugged. He didn't like the fact that a woman had almost taken him down.

He wasn't a chauvinist, but he *was* a trained fighter and had outweighed that woman by probably a hundred pounds.

However, he *had* been incapacitated in his current state. Still, his ego would be bruised for a while.

"I'm not sure who she was working for." Monroe fought a grimace as he shifted in bed.

"What did she say?" Charlie pulled up a chair and sat beside him.

"I asked who she was, and she told me it wasn't important. That I should have backed off."

"From what?"

"That's what I asked. Then she said, 'I think you and I both know the answer to that question,' and that she'd be back."

A frown tugged at Charlie's lips. "I'm so glad things turned out the way they did instead of how the woman planned. I don't suppose you've heard any updates from the police?"

Knowing Charlie, she'd probably tapped into her contacts with the local police, and she already knew about any updates.

But Monroe would humor her. "I heard they checked the security camera footage, but they haven't gotten any matches in their system. People saw this woman leaving the hospital, but she was able to slip away and jump into a vehicle—the car was reported stolen last night. She abandoned it about two miles from here in an area without any security cameras. Someone else must have picked her up from there."

"In other words, the woman was a professional." Charlie frowned again.

Monroe squeezed her hand with both of his. "It sounds like someone is desperate to silence both of us."

"Yes, it seems that way."

He didn't like seeing that forlorn look in her eyes, one that was filled with worry.

Charlie had a lot of responsibility on her shoulders. She handled everything with so much ease and grace. But perhaps the latest turn of events were beginning to tear her down.

Monroe shifted in bed, trying to think of a way to cheer her up.

Only one thing came to mind. "I do have some good news for you."

Her countenance seemed to lift at his words. "What's that?"

"The doctor said I might be able to go home in a couple of days."

Her eyes brightened. "Really? I thought it was still a week out, at least."

"The doctor and I had a long heart-to-heart." In truth, Monroe had insisted that he leave as soon as possible.

The doctor had finally capitulated and admitted that a week might not be necessary.

"That's great." Charlie squeezed his hand.

"He said I'm progressing well and he thinks I'll

progress even faster once I'm somewhere more comfortable. Most of the medications and therapies I need I'll be able to handle on my own. I'll just need to come in for a follow-up, of course."

"Of course," Charlie said. "You're right, that is some of the best news I've heard in a long time."

But questions continued to swirl in Monroe's head. Had someone connected with the Overland Hotel bombing discovered that he and Charlie were getting closer to answers? Had this person decided to strike Monroe, knowing that if he were harmed it could derail Charlie?

He wasn't sure.

But he was even more determined to protect Charlie and help her find the answers she needed.

That was why he had to heal as quickly as possible.

Because in his current state, Monroe wasn't good for anything.

CHARLIE WATCHED the dust fly around them as their helicopter landed at Vanishing Ranch.

The property was located in the western part of Arizona, and she had originally started with two hundred acres. Recently, she'd purchased eight hundred more acres, thanks to some generous grants by donors. Those donors were mostly rich friends of her father's who liked to stay in touch and support what she was doing.

Normally, people walked from the helicopter to the buildings at the ranch. But Charlie wanted to give Monroe more time to rebuild his strength before she asked him to do that. That's why a Humvee pulled onto the scene, Mateo—one of her operatives— behind the wheel.

As the blades stopped, she turned to Monroe and pulled her headset off. "You ready for this?"

"I've been ready."

She flashed a grin before climbing from the copter and hurrying around to his side as he descended. She really wanted to put her arm around him to make sure he was okay. But she wouldn't emasculate him by trying to help him out.

Instead, she remained close, ready to act if he asked.

They climbed into the Humvee and settled in the back while Mateo drove them toward the small house Charlie called home.

"We missed you around here, man." Mateo glanced at them in the rearview mirror.

"I've missed being here." Monroe glanced out the window. "Am I staying in the clinic? Or at my place?"

"Neither," Charlie said. "You're staying at my place."

He raised his eyebrows as he stared at her. "Your place? People might talk."

"Then let them. There's no way you're staying alone, and I don't trust anyone else to take care of you other than myself."

"Okay then." His eyebrows remained raised, but

he knew better than to argue. "Is Amberly okay with this?"

A rock formed in Charlie's chest at the mention of her daughter. "I didn't ask her permission."

Monroe didn't say anything, but Charlie knew he had thoughts on the situation. He'd been her sounding board and offered advice—but only when she asked.

She picked a piece of fuzz from his shirt and plucked it onto the floor.

"You don't have to fuss over me, you know," Monroe muttered.

"Of course I do." She grinned at him, and he gave her a knowing look in return.

After Mateo pulled to a stop, Charlie and Monroe climbed out.

A crowd gathered around the Hummer and began clapping.

Charlie saw the semblance of a smile tugging at Monroe's lips as the welcoming crew cheered him on.

He meant more to the people around here than he realized.

Charlie's gaze scanned the crowd, which was mostly comprised of her operatives. Jesse and Sienna. Hudson, Teagan, and their baby. Mateo. Hayes. Ainsley. Chef and Kota. Even Natalie and Joshua were here.

She fondly called this crew "Charlie's Angels." She thought the name was appropriate because they were all a huge blessing to her.

Charlie's gaze stopped when she saw Amberly lingering in the back.

The fifteen-year-old—she'd just had a birthday two weeks ago—scowled at Charlie before stomping away.

The rock in Charlie's chest seemed to grow larger by the moment.

She'd talked to Amberly's tutor again on the way here and knew Amberly was giving the woman a hard time. The teen didn't want to do her assignments or listen to a word Vanessa told her.

Charlie wasn't happy with the update.

She turned back to Monroe and placed a hand on his arm. "You'll all have plenty of time to catch up with Monroe later. For now, I'm going to have to be the bad guy. We need to get him settled so he can rest some more."

As the crowd dispersed, she led Monroe across the dry, dusty ground to her house, which was located at the back of the property. The plot of land offered more privacy and was located the farthest away from all the other buildings.

Eight guesthouses lined one side of the property, and the stables and bunkhouse were on the other side. Forefront to the entry gate was the mess hall, which also contained offices, a conference area, a workout room, and a small medical clinic.

A pool glimmered in front of the guesthouses as well as other adornments from when this place had been a dude ranch—including an old stagecoach.

Behind the buildings stretched a large pasture for the horses—there were fourteen in all.

The place practically felt like a desert paradise—most of the time.

However, Charlie was running out of room. Her operatives usually stayed in the bunkhouse—there was a male and a female side with a common area in the middle.

But now more of her operatives were getting married. She'd had to put some modular units between the ranch itself and the new lodge being built on the property. Legacy Lodge, when it was done, would house victims of human trafficking.

Jesse and Sienna stayed in one of those modulars, and Hudson and Teagan stayed in another.

Charlie had a feeling there would be more marriages soon, however.

She was trying to keep on top of the lodging situation, but everything out here in the desert took longer to build than it did other places. The area was secluded and without the resources that incorporated communities had.

Charlie paused and unlocked the door to her place.

She'd get Monroe settled and then go talk to Amberly, she decided. Charlie had to iron this thing out with the private tutor.

The ranch had hired a different on-call tutor to help their guests who came here with children.

Amberly needed someone permanent.

After vetting several candidates, Charlie had finally hired a woman named Vanessa Owens. She was a recent college graduate who'd studied both education and equine therapy.

She was a perfect fit here at the ranch.

Out here in the middle of the desert, no schools were close. Besides, Charlie wouldn't trust leaving Amberly at school. It would be risky for more than one reason.

In addition to Vanessa, Charlie had also tasked Ainsley with keeping an eye on Amberly while Charlie was gone.

She couldn't leave the girl here alone without a guardian. In fact, she wouldn't have left the teen at all except for the fact that Monroe had been critically injured.

However, Charlie worried about the girl. She'd

been dropped off at the ranch a few months ago after her adoptive parents died, and she was having trouble dealing with the changes in her life. Charlie had tried to talk to her, to be there for her.

But Amberly wanted nothing to do with her, and Charlie felt as if she was hitting her head against the wall.

Monroe kept telling her that she needed to give it more time.

But Charlie liked to fix things in a timely manner. However, her relationship with Amberly felt beyond repair.

She let out a sigh as she pushed open the door to her house.

For now, she needed to concentrate on Monroe.

———

Monroe paused as he stepped inside Charlie's house.

He'd been inside many times before but never as an overnight guest. He knew Charlie was letting him stay simply to be practical. The doctor had said he shouldn't be alone for at least the first week after being released from the hospital.

But he felt unusually nervous . . . and intrigued.

"The couch will work." He nodded to the brown leather sofa in the center of the space.

Charlie scooted in front of him. "Don't be ridiculous. You're going to take my room. I already had Kota change the sheets for you. I just need to grab a few things, and then you can have some privacy. You'll be much more comfortable there."

"I can't take your room, Charlie." He took a step back and shook his head.

"Of course you can. I insist."

He knew that tone of voice. Knew there was no use in arguing when Charlie used it.

But he still didn't like the idea of taking over her space.

She took his arm and led him into the room.

He'd never seen her bedroom before, but it looked surprisingly feminine with its white curtains, white bedspread, and iron-framed bed.

It wasn't that Charlie wasn't feminine—she most definitely was. But she liked to keep up a tough appearance, so the gentle decorations surprised him.

He wondered what else about Charlie might surprise him.

Charlie turned toward him, her eye still black from whatever encounter she'd had.

Even with a black eye, she was still the most gorgeous woman Monroe had ever laid eyes on.

"Now, the doctor said you needed to get plenty of

rest so you can't jump into things too quickly." Her bossy gaze met his.

Monroe put his hands on her shoulders. "Charlie, you've got to stop worrying about me."

Some type of emotion quivered in her gaze. "How can I *not* worry about you?"

He waited for Charlie to continue. Was she worried about him because she cared? Would this be the moment when she told him that?

He nearly held his breath.

"I mean, you are officially my employee," she finished with a hard swallow. "I'm responsible for you."

Monroe's heart fell.

Of course.

Her *employee*.

He'd always liked to think of himself as so much more.

Yet he often reminded himself that he'd be foolish to ever let himself get his hopes up.

"Now that you mention it, I *am* feeling tired." He nodded toward the bed. "Maybe I'll lie down for a while. When I wake up, I'll bring some of my things over so I can take a shower and change."

"That's a great idea—but I'll have someone bring your things for you." Charlie nodded in agreement.

"After that, I can bring you some dinner. Does that work?"

"That sounds perfect."

He walked toward the bed and paused, looking back at her one more time as the ache in his heart seemed to grow stronger. "Thanks for everything you've done for me, Charlie."

She flashed an unreadable smile back at him. "Of course."

He had to find a way to get over this woman before his heart was crushed . . . again.

Except this time, he might not be able to put the pieces back together.

CHAPTER
NINE

AS CHARLIE CLOSED the door to Monroe's room, her heart pounded against her chest.

She didn't want to leave him. But she had too many things to juggle at the moment.

Usually, she considered herself a good multi-tasker. Right now, she felt on the verge of dropping everything and watching all that was important to her crash and shatter at her feet.

First, Amberly had shown up unexpectedly a few months ago. The teen's appearance had thrown Charlie off her game, to say the least.

Then the new lodge she was building had come under attack.

But when Monroe got hurt . . . all her problems seemed to triple.

Charlie sighed. Right now, she needed to talk to Amberly.

She stepped out of her house and closed the door before glancing around.

Daisy, a corgi who'd become the unofficial ranch dog, raced up to her, tail wagging, and waited patiently for a pat on the head.

"I can always count on you to be happy to see me," Charlie murmured.

The dog rubbed herself on Charlie's leg before scampering off to greet someone else.

Charlie had only taken a few more steps when she ran into Teagan Carmichael.

Teagan was Hudson's wife, and she had her three-month-old baby boy, Crew, in her arms. Charlie stopped a moment to fawn over the beautiful child.

She was thrilled to see her employees here at the ranch flourishing. The men and women she'd hired loved what they did. They all seemed to love ranch life as well.

She was on the verge of needing to hire more people, but she had to figure out the housing situation first.

She hadn't expected Vanishing Ranch to grow so quickly.

"Have you seen Amberly?" Charlie asked.

Teagan nodded toward the stable. "Last time I saw her, she was heading in there."

Irritation pinched Charlie's spine.

She knew the girl liked horses.

But she also knew the girl liked Jonathan, the eighteen-year-old ranch hand Charlie had hired not long ago. The boy seemed responsible enough, and he definitely knew about horses. Charlie had hired him as a favor to a former colleague; Jonathan was his nephew.

Right now, she was keeping the teen on a short leash until he proved himself.

Wasting no more time, Charlie stormed toward the barn. She opened the door—it was surprisingly quiet as it rolled on the track above it—and stepped inside the dark space.

She walked down the center aisle, rubbing the noses of several horses as she did.

Amberly was nowhere to be seen.

But if not here, then where?

Charlie continued pacing before pausing near the stall at the end.

Two people leaned against the back wall, so caught up in their embrace that they didn't even hear Charlie.

Probably because they were . . . kissing. *Really* kissing.

Tension knitted between her shoulders.

What had she just walked into?

———

Charlie's heart skipped a beat when she recognized the woman's dark hair. "Amberly?"

Amberly and Jonathan flew apart.

But her daughter didn't even have the decency to look embarrassed as she glanced back at Charlie. Instead, she almost appeared glad she'd been caught.

Anger simmered inside Charlie at the realization.

Jonathan, on the other hand, avoided eye contact and tried to blend in with the shadows.

Too late.

Charlie pointed at Jonathan. "You!"

"I'm . . . I'm sorry, Ms. Soldier."

"We need to have a serious talk later. For now, get out of here."

The ranch hand didn't hesitate. He darted from the stall and out of sight.

Then Charlie turned to Amberly. "You need to get to the house so we can talk. Now."

She said nothing to the girl as they walked back to the house. Charlie would save everything she had to say until they had some privacy.

Inside, Amberly plopped down on the couch and

stared at her, waiting with crossed arms for whatever Charlie had to say.

The girl had a defiant gaze, raven-colored hair, and was a real head turner. She was also very persuasive.

She was basically Charlie's clone—which could explain why the two of them kept butting heads.

"What were you thinking?" Charlie demanded as she planted herself in front of the teen.

"I was thinking that I like Jonathan." Amberly offered a smug smile.

Irritation pinched Charlie's spine. "I told you to stay away from him."

"If he's such a bad guy, then why did you hire him?"

"He's not a bad guy. That's not the point. The point is that I told you to stay away."

Amberly shrugged, defiance still stretching through her gaze. "There's nothing else to do around here. Do you expect me to kick rocks all day and play with horses?"

"Look, I know it's not an easy life out here. I'm sorry about that. I know you want to be around kids your own age, and I'm trying to find a solution. But neither of us expected to be in this situation."

"No, you never expected to see me again, did you?" Accusation dripped from Amberly's voice.

Charlie repressed a sigh. She'd heard these allegations before.

Every time, the words still hurt.

"You know it's not like that." Charlie softened her voice. "I was young when I had you, and I knew I couldn't give you the life you deserved. Your mom and dad were wonderful people, and I knew you'd have a good life with them."

"I guess you just never counted on the fact that they both could be dead before I reached fifteen."

Charlie lowered herself into a chair adjacent to the couch, already feeling exhausted. "Of course I never thought that."

The two had died in a tragic boating accident, leaving Amberly parentless.

Amberly continued to scowl. "And you never thought about staying in touch?"

Charlie had wondered when these topics would come up. But Amberly had avoided this conversation whenever Charlie tried to talk to her.

Maybe the fact that Charlie had been away for almost two weeks had caused a change in her.

"I *did* think about it," Charlie said. "It was complicated, and I didn't want your life to be complicated. I kept tabs on you from a distance. You seemed happy. And I knew when the day came, if you ever wanted to meet with me, that I'd be open to it. I just didn't expect it to happen like this."

Amberly's expression remained tight, and she appeared as if she didn't believe anything Charlie said. But Charlie didn't miss the moisture brimming in the teen's eyes.

A pang of compassion captured her heart.

Lord . . . give me the right words to say. Please.

She cleared her throat. "Amberly, we've both got to make the most of things."

"That's what I was trying to do . . . with Jonathan." Her voice hardened again.

Charlie knew the girl was coming from a place of hurt and grief. Her defiance only masked those other emotions. But Charlie couldn't be disrespected like this.

It would set a bad precedent for the future if she allowed it. Still, she'd have to proceed carefully.

Charlie leaned closer. "Please don't make the same mistakes that I did."

The girl's eyebrows flew up. "And what kind of mistakes were those exactly?"

Charlie licked her lips as she considered how much to say.

CHAPTER
TEN

MONROE TRIED NOT to eavesdrop as he lay in bed.

But it was hard not to. The walls weren't very thick in this house.

He wasn't sure Charlie realized exactly how loudly she was talking. Amberly, on the other hand, probably didn't care.

Monroe wished he could tune out the conversation and put some earbuds in. But not only did he not have any earbuds, he was curious too.

He and Charlie had known each other a long time. They'd talked about a lot of things.

But Charlie's past wasn't something she brought up very often.

"Amberly . . ." Charlie started, her voice muted

on the other side of the door. "After my dad died, I went through a truly rebellious stage."

"Your dad being football superstar Benjamin Soldier?" Amberly's voice contained a mocking tone.

"That's right. During football season and training I didn't see him often. But when we were together, he was the best dad I could ask for. When I lost him, I felt like I lost my whole world. I'd just lost my grandmother less than a year before that."

"But you still had your mom." An accusatory tone captured Amberly's voice.

"I did, but my dad's death devastated her, and she became a shell of who she used to be. I felt like I was left with no one. So I turned to guys to fill the void. I knew I was pretty, and I knew I could get almost any guy I wanted. So I did. And I did foolish things."

"Like getting pregnant?"

"That certainly wasn't part of my plan." Charlie's voice sounded strained.

"So, I'm a mistake?"

"That's not what I said," Charlie murmured. "I don't believe God makes mistakes. You're a beautiful young lady, and you're a blessing. But, like I said, I wasn't in the place to be a mom. I was too lost myself, and I would've just taken you down the wrong path with me."

"And my father? I asked Mom and Dad about him once, but no one seemed to know who he is."

Monroe swallowed hard, again knowing he shouldn't listen.

Charlie had never told him about Amberly. He hadn't even known she had a child until Amberly showed up at Vanishing Ranch one day.

Since then, he'd wondered about that part of Charlie's story. Had wondered exactly who Amberly's dad was. He had no idea.

He turned over in bed, determined to tune out the conversation.

But he couldn't.

"What about him?" Charlie asked.

"Does he even know about me?"

"That's a long story."

"Who is he?" Amberly demanded.

There was a pause.

"I . . . I can't tell you that," Charlie finally muttered. "Not right now."

She almost sounded nervous, Monroe mused.

"Why not?" Amberly demanded.

"There's a lot to it. You're not ready to hear the story yet."

More questions raced through Monroe's mind.

There was so much about Charlie he didn't know yet.

But he wanted to know it all.

Would Charlie ever let him in?

Monroe punched the pillow beneath him again, unsure of that answer.

———

After Charlie and Amberly finished their conversation, Charlie told Amberly to work on her homework.

Amberly hadn't been happy about it, but she'd stomped off to her room, closed the door a little too loudly, and Charlie hadn't heard from her since.

Maybe Monroe staying at her place wouldn't be as restful for him as Charlie had hoped.

She nearly collapsed in her armchair, her face buried in her hands as she remembered the painful conversation she'd just had with her daughter.

Charlie had never intended on being a mother. She'd known giving Amberly up for adoption was the best thing for both of them. She'd never anticipated raising her.

But God must have brought Amberly back into her life for a reason.

Yet she felt as if she was failing at every step of the way.

Should she give up everything she'd worked for

here at Vanishing Ranch and devote all her time and attention to Amberly?

Certainly, that wasn't what God was calling her to do . . . was it? Charlie had invested so much in this place and in helping victims who needed a fresh start.

Much of the reason she'd started this place was because of her own mother.

After Charlie's father had died, her mom remarried.

Charlie had never liked the man, and she'd told her mom that. Charlie didn't like the way the guy looked at her. Didn't like the fact that he was so obsessed with her father's money.

Brian had just moved right into their lives and had taken over.

Thankfully, her dad had set Charlie up with her own account—that way Brian wouldn't be able to take everything and wipe out that part of her dad's legacy.

But her mom ignored Charlie's concerns about the man. Blamed her feelings on the grief and jealousy Charlie was experiencing.

A month into her mother's marriage, Charlie heard them having their first fight.

Then the argument got violent.

Eventually, Charlie realized that Brian was slapping her mom around on a regular basis.

She'd begged her mom to leave him.

Her mom had refused. Instead, her mother had made excuses for him. Claimed he was just having a bad day, or that he was sorry, or that he'd promised he wouldn't do it again.

Finally, Charlie made the choice to leave the situation. She couldn't be around the abuse any longer. It had begun to affect her also.

Thankfully, Wallace and Greta Masterson had found her several months later—after Charlie had hit the lowest point of her life—and they'd helped her back onto her feet.

Six months after living with Wallace and Greta, Charlie had contacted her mom.

But her mom didn't want to reconcile.

She'd even said she was glad that Charlie was out of the house. Had said Charlie only ever caused her heartache.

Charlie's heart had shattered at her words.

Her mom had chosen Brian, her abuser, over her.

Charlie hadn't understood at the time. But now she understood the control abusers had over their victims. She'd forgiven her mom.

Charlie had no choice but to move forward. At twenty-one, she'd been able to access the trust fund her father had left her. He'd made a good living with the NFL, and he'd also done endorsement deals for a clothing company, an airline, and a sports drink company.

She knew, if she was wise, she'd never have to work a day in her life.

Wallace had been financially savvy. He knew the stock market and taught her how to invest wisely.

Before he'd died, he'd even set up an endowment just for Vanishing Ranch. That endowment helped with her operating costs and kept her afloat.

Wallace and Greta had lived on a horse farm, and Charlie had fallen in love with the creatures. So, when the opportunity had arisen, she'd purchased an old dude ranch in Arizona so she could rescue horses.

Everyone had thought she was crazy for doing so.

But she had a bigger plan—one that had taken years to implement.

She wanted to help women who were in the same situation as her mother. Who needed to escape. To start fresh.

The government put people in witness protection—but not abused women. They were on their own.

Charlie didn't like that there were so few options for the average, everyday hurting person.

So she'd decided to hire the best of the best to help her with her new mission.

Then she'd met with lawyers and other people in the know so she could figure out how to set up people with new identities and careers. The task hadn't been easy, but she knew she couldn't jump into this without doing the proper research first.

She'd also begun speaking around the country about her father's legacy and building up connections she needed. She'd found she was good at it and that people were looking for something to believe in—something like a horse rescue that would also one day serve as a place of equine therapy.

Much of the other details had to remain under wraps, however.

Privacy and security were keys of her organization.

Finally, three years ago, her full vision for Vanishing Ranch had come to fruition.

She'd begun helping women get fresh starts with new identities, new jobs, and new places to live—but that was only after they went through counseling and job training to ensure they had the emotional stability and skills they needed to make it on their own.

As Charlie sat in the chair, she lifted her head and

ran a hand through her hair. Then she touched next to her eye. The skin there was still tender.

She sighed.

She couldn't sit here and feel sorry for herself.

Not when there was so much work to be done.

And not when she needed a crash course in parenting a teenager.

CHAPTER
ELEVEN

AS AFTERNOON TURNED INTO EVENING, Monroe heard the knock at his door and called, "Come in."

Charlie stepped inside with a tray in her hands. "I've got dinner."

He started to sit up. He'd already taken a shower and changed into some fresh clothes Charlie had brought in for him. But he must have drifted back to sleep.

"Stay right where you are," Charlie called. "I can set this tray on your lap, and you can relax."

He could get used to having someone take care of him like this. But if he were smart, he wouldn't.

He'd been married before to a woman named Kennedy. They'd met when he'd played professional football.

Monroe had been a different person back then. Into partying and social status and material wealth. Kennedy had been the same.

Eventually, he began to reap the fruits of that kind of life—the rotten fruits. He made poor decisions. His health began to decline because of his drinking. Even with all the money he brought in, he found himself in debt because of the lavish lifestyle he and Kennedy were living.

Then, after waking up from being passed out at a party, he'd met Benjamin Soldier.

The man had been his hero—a real football icon and role model.

Benjamin had seen the dangerous path Monroe was going down and tried to help him.

At first, Monroe hadn't listened. He'd been too caught up in trying not to lose everything he'd worked so hard for.

Then a knee injury had taken him out of the game, and Monroe had hit rock bottom.

Benjamin, instead of scoffing at him for rejecting his help earlier, had been there for him.

Monroe had slowly begun to make changes in his life—in his spending, his social circles, his alcohol consumption. He knew he had to turn his life around. He'd even started going to church.

Kennedy, however, hadn't liked those changes. She didn't want her life to be different. She couldn't handle the fact their money was drying up.

Three months after being benched, Monroe caught her having an affair with one of his friends.

Kennedy hadn't wanted to work things out with him. Monroe hadn't been sure he'd wanted to either, not after that kind of betrayal.

So they'd gotten divorced.

He'd left the NFL.

He'd gone back to school. Got a degree in business. Then he'd opened a private security firm, one that primarily did bodyguard jobs for politicians and celebrities.

At first, he worked in the field. Eventually, he hired enough people that he could work as an administrator.

Several years down the line, when Charlie had approached him about working for her . . . he hadn't been able to say no.

He'd sold his business to his second in command, and he'd moved to Arizona.

He snapped from his thoughts as Charlie carefully placed the tray over his legs and then pulled the cloche off the plate. "It's your favorite. Chinese food."

His stomach grumbled when he saw it. "Chinese food? Where did you get that way out here?"

"Would you believe me if I said I called in for takeout?"

"Not at all. It would be cold by the time it got here."

She chuckled then walked to the other side of the bed and plopped down on top of the covers beside him. "I asked Chef if he'd make it for you."

The sweet and spicy scent of General Tso's chicken and fried rice floated up to him. It smelled heavenly. There were even three egg rolls on his plate.

"I'll have to tell him thank you." He lifted a quick prayer before grabbing the chopsticks. "Did you eat?"

"I'm not hungry."

"Have you eaten today?" He worried about Charlie sometimes—a *lot* of the time, actually.

She was so busy taking care of other people that she often forgot to take care of herself.

"I grabbed a few things here and there." She shrugged.

In other words, no. She hadn't had a decent meal.

He pushed the plate closer. "Have some. I insist. My stomach's not ready for all this anyway."

She plucked an eggroll from his plate. "Maybe I will have one."

Monroe took a few bites before turning to her. "Are you ready to update me yet on everything I've missed?"

A slight frown tugged at her lips. "Maybe I should let you eat first."

"There's no reason to keep delaying this."

Still holding her eggroll, she leaned back, adjusting a pillow behind her.

Then she began to detail everything that had happened since his accident, bouncing the uneaten eggroll in the air to drive home each point.

She told him about discovering who the Hollises really were.

Finding the link with editor Margaret Creighton.

What Margaret had told her.

How the editor had then gone into cardiac arrest when an intruder broke into her home.

When Charlie finished updating him, she took a bite of her eggroll. She ate the whole thing in five bites and then wiped her hands on a napkin and leaned back.

Monroe's appetite was gone, so he set his chopsticks down as he processed all the updates. "I don't like the way this sounds."

"I know." Charlie pulled her knees toward her

chest as she stared straight ahead, looking more like a teenager than a thirty-one-year-old woman. "But I feel like we're getting closer to answers."

"Clearly, we are. These people wouldn't be coming after us if we weren't."

"All these conspiracies we've come up with about why the Overland Hotel bombing really took place . . . one of them isn't actually a conspiracy. It's the truth. Former President Radar has something to do with all of this."

Monroe gave her a reassuring glance. "You'll figure it out. I know you will."

Charlie turned toward him, still resting her head against the pillow behind her. "What I need is to make sure that you get better."

"I'm working on it."

She continued to study his face. Monroe tried to ignore her scrutiny as he took a sip of his water, but it was hard when Charlie was right there. And so close.

And so . . . beautiful.

"Did you hear my conversation with Amberly?" Her voice sounded strained.

Her question snapped Monroe from his thoughts.

He swallowed hard, knowing he couldn't lie to her. "I heard a few things. I wasn't trying but . . ."

She nodded, unoffended—and not appearing surprised either. "I know there are parts of my story that I've never told you. I'm sorry you had to hear them that way."

"They're your stories to share. It's okay."

Charlie reached up and touched his jaw again, her fingers gently stroking his face—just like she'd done in the hospital. "You are a remarkable man, Monroe Davis."

Shivers raced through him at her touch. "I think you're pretty remarkable too."

His heart thumped harder, and he suddenly forgot all about his food.

All he could think about was the fact that Charlie was staring at him with such a warm, soft look in her eyes.

A look she usually reserved just for him.

Everyone else knew Charlie as being hard-core. But around Monroe, she loosened up. Showed more of her vulnerabilities. Her softer side.

He considered that a real gift.

As their gazes locked, all Monroe wanted was to lean closer. To finally know what it would feel like if their lips touched.

Was that what she wanted too? Or was all of this simply a gesture of friendship?

Her hand remained at his jaw and their gazes on each other.

Something silent passed between them.

An ache formed in his chest, clawing for relief. An ache to desperately know Charlie more.

Monroe thought she wanted the same thing.

Life wasn't anything without taking some risks, right?

He'd held back for so long. He was quiet, but he wasn't shy. However, his friendship with Charlie was too important to mess up.

Still . . .

"Charlie . . ." he murmured.

"Yes?"

He leaned closer, and Charlie's eyes closed.

She wanted this kiss too, didn't she?

Before their lips touched, a knock jerked them both from the moment.

They propelled themselves away from each other as if shoved by an unseen force. The plate clattered on the tray as Monroe's knees jolted up. Charlie's hand went over her heart.

The moment was broken.

Just in time.

Maybe that was God's way of saying that kiss had been a bad idea.

––––––––

What was Charlie thinking? She'd almost kissed Monroe.

Monroe was different from the other guys she'd had in her life.

Yet that was what scared her. She would never, ever put herself in a position again where she was at the mercy of a man.

She knew that Monroe would never ask her to do that either.

Her emotions and logic warred inside her.

She quickly stood from the bed and brushed off her jeans.

It was better that kiss hadn't happened, no matter what argument her heart made.

"I need to answer that," she rushed, nodding toward the door.

Monroe straightened up the tray where some rice and chicken had spilled. "Of course."

Charlie smoothed her hair, hoping that she didn't look as disheveled as she felt when she answered the door.

Jesse stood outside. The look in his eyes made it clear he had something urgent to tell her.

"The state police are here," he announced stiffly.

Alarm raced through her. "What?"

"They want to talk to you."

"How many?"

"There are four cars on the other side of the gate. Some of the women are freaking out."

She drew in a deep breath. "Assure them that everything's going to be okay. They should go inside their guesthouses and close the doors until I tell them it's safe to come out. Okay? Get the other guys to help you spread the message. And do it on the down low so the police don't see us. Got it?"

"Got it."

She rushed back to Monroe to share the update with him.

"I heard." Monroe was already starting to get out of bed.

"Stay where you are," Charlie insisted. "I'll get you if I need you. Right now, I need you to heal so I can use you later. I'll be fine. Okay?"

Monroe hesitated until the truth about his current state rolled through his gaze, and he nodded. "Okay."

After pulling on her black leather jacket and boots, Charlie strode outside and across the dusty landscape toward the gate surrounding the property.

Blue and red flashing lights lit the otherwise dark air. Clearly, the cops hadn't shown up with their sirens on. She was thankful for that at least.

But a detective stood at the gate, appearing rather impatient with his hands on his hips.

"What can I help you gentlemen with?" Charlie paused near the gate, not opening it.

"Detective Vincent." The man with thick salt-and-pepper hair, wearing a button-up shirt and dark slacks, held up a badge. "Someone filed a complaint against you."

"Did they now? You brought four vehicles with you when you came here to tell me?"

His gaze narrowed. "We'd like to come in."

Charlie hesitated, wondering the best way to handle this. She took a deep breath, determined to keep her cool. It was what she did best.

Wallace had taught her the importance of keeping her emotions under control. He'd told her she'd get much further in life if she did so—especially if she wanted to work with men who often saw emotions as weakness.

She'd always remembered that advice—among many other things he'd taught her.

She quickly surveyed the situation.

These weren't the local sheriff's deputies. She'd met most of them before. She also had contacts with most of the law enforcement agencies in the area.

Someone from there would have given her a heads-up before showing up here.

These guys were from the Arizona Department of Public Safety, CID—criminal investigations division.

Charlie hadn't dealt with them before.

She swallowed hard before asking, "What kind of complaint are we talking about?"

Detective Vincent locked gazes with her. "Someone reported that this place is involved with human trafficking."

CHAPTER
TWELVE

DESPITE CHARLIE'S INSTRUCTIONS, Monroe lumbered out of bed and stepped outside. He saw the lights flashing in the distance.

What in the world was going on?

His hands fisted at his sides. More than anything, he wanted to be out there. He wanted to hear what was going on. He wanted to help.

But at the thought of that, his side began to ache and reminded him of his injuries.

He wasn't ready to jump into the action yet, no matter how much he wanted to.

If he injured himself again in his current state, he might not recover. Then he wouldn't be any good to anyone. At least, that was how it felt.

As his cell phone rang, he glanced at the screen.

It was William Tate.

Monroe had called William, one of his contacts, and asked him to investigate the woman who attacked him in the hospital. William worked as a liaison between law enforcement agencies, so he was privy to such information. The two of them had played professional football together and had remained friends.

William was also one of only a handful of people who knew the truth about what they did at Vanishing Ranch. But, as with most of their contacts, they'd been instructed to deny their knowledge if they were ever questioned.

"Hey, William." Monroe kept his gaze fixated on the scene in the distance.

"I think I found out something for you."

"I could use some good news."

"I found a picture of the woman who attacked you at the hospital, and I ran her image through several facial recognition programs," he started. "I got a match. Her name is Delilah Perkins. Ring any bells?"

He searched his memories but came up with nothing. "I can't say it does."

"She works for an organization called Dagger."

His breath caught when he heard the name. "I thought they'd disbanded."

Dagger was a private security group that took on

less than scrupulous jobs. Their leader had been busted more than a year ago, so Monroe thought that was the end of the organization.

He'd dealt with the private agents on a couple of occasions when he'd owned his protection services business.

"Apparently, the agency found a way to pull themselves back together, despite their troubles," William said. "Anyway, this woman is former Army, and she was recruited to work for Dagger about six months ago. Not surprisingly, she was kicked out of the military for misconduct. She was constantly starting trouble."

Monroe shifted and settled against the house. "Sounds about right. Any idea where this Delilah woman is now?"

"She's in the wind. So be careful. If someone hired her to finish you off, she might not stop until she succeeds."

His stomach clenched at William's admonition. "Got it. Thanks for your help. I really appreciate it."

"Anytime."

———

Charlie knew if she denied these officers entrance too long that they'd come back with even more men, with more fuel in the fire, and that they could do even more damage.

The more she fought them, the more guilty she'd look.

Instead, she punched in her code and opened the gate. The arms slowly swung out.

"Leave your cars out there, but you can come in on foot," Charlie instructed. "And don't disturb any of my guests. They're off-limits."

"Guests?" Detective Vincent joined her, and they began pacing toward the center of the property.

"That's right."

"This place isn't listed as a hotel. There are no permits for that."

"When I said guests, I meant *guests*. Not customers. They're people I've invited to stay for a while. I'm not running a secret business, detective."

His eyes narrowed. "Who are these so-called guests then?"

"People who are fascinated with horses and the Old West and the desert. This is a wonderful place. Why not share it with people I've met along the way?"

The man stared at Charlie another moment as if he didn't believe her.

As the rest of the men flooded the space, apprehension rose inside her.

This could turn ugly quickly. The only comfort Charlie found was in the fact that her operatives were all nearby. They all dressed like cowboys, and they took turns caring for the horses, which helped them blend in and look like ranch hands instead of former law enforcement and military.

That should work in their favor right now.

Plus, they were experienced. They knew how to handle themselves in situations like this.

But she couldn't deny the thrum of nerves she felt.

As she watched the men walking throughout the ranch, her gaze met Ainsley's.

Charlie knew by looking at the woman that she was worried also.

She glanced in the distance and saw Monroe standing outside her place, watching everything from there.

Normally, he'd be by her side. Charlie missed his presence entirely too much.

All this self-talk she'd been giving herself about not depending on a man was an illusion.

She'd been in denial.

Because she *had* been depending on Monroe for a long time. She just hadn't realized it until she'd nearly lost him.

As she and the detective stopped outside the mess hall, Detective Vincent turned toward her.

"We're going to need to talk to these guests of yours." He said the word *guests* as if Charlie were hiding something.

Which she was. But she couldn't show that on her face.

"Like I said earlier, I respect my guests' privacy," she started. "And I'm not going to let you enter their places without a warrant."

"That can be arranged." He stepped closer, clearly trying to intimidate her. "What are you hiding, Charlie Soldier?"

She refused to break his gaze. "Nothing. I'm not hiding anything."

"I don't believe you." He glared down at her.

She raised her chin, determined to keep her composure. "Who made this so-called complaint against me?"

"I'm not at liberty to say."

Anger ignited inside Charlie, but she held her emotions back. "That's because whoever made it was a coward. No one around here has ever complained to my face. Most of the people in this area appreciate what I'm doing. Appreciate the fact that I rescue horses and nurse them back to health."

"I have no doubt that you're doing that." Vincent

narrowed his eyes. "My question is, what else are you doing?"

His query hung in the air.

Certain people knew the truth about what Charlie did—carefully chosen people she'd picked to be in her network. She needed them to help identify women who needed help.

But if Charlie told too many people, then this place would no longer be a safe haven.

She couldn't risk that.

Detective Vincent continued to stare at her a few moments before rounding up the other officers.

Charlie half expected him to tell her not to leave town.

Instead, she watched as they walked toward their vehicles without another word and climbed back inside. As soon as she could, Charlie closed the gate and made sure it was secure.

Then she remained at the fence and watched until the vehicles disappeared from sight.

She didn't know if Detective Vincent could secure a search warrant, but she was certain he would try.

Until then, she'd just have to be vigilant.

Because either way, Charlie knew this was far from over.

MONROE STOOD with Charlie outside her place and listened as she talked to Jesse and Hudson—two of her most trusted operatives.

Actually, Monroe knew she trusted everyone she employed here. She had some real stand-up men and women working for her—the best of the best.

"Jesse, I need you to look into Detective Vincent." Charlie effortlessly switched into boss mode. "He's in someone's pocket. I'm sure of it. It's the only reason the police would have come out here tonight. Someone wants to intimidate us."

"I agree." Jesse nodded, his gaze dark as if he didn't like any of this either. "Who sent him? Who's really pulling the strings here?"

"The person who wants to shut down our investigation." Monroe crossed his arms and scowled.

"Radar?" Jesse glanced between Charlie and Monroe.

Charlie shrugged. "He's powerful enough, and he has the connections."

"Who else could it be?" Hudson adjusted the cowboy hat atop his head and shifted.

"That's what we need to figure out." Charlie shook her head, her gaze steely, before she doled out more instructions.

Monroe studied her a moment.

She looked overwhelmed—her eyelids heavy, her lips slightly downturned, her skin paler than usual.

She had so much on her plate right now. He only wished he wasn't one of those burdens.

But he knew that he was.

Taking care of him hadn't been something Charlie had planned on doing. No matter how many times she told him that she wanted to help nurse him back to health, he felt like he was in the way.

He turned as the door to Charlie's place opened and Amberly stepped out.

His heart had gone out to the girl from the moment he'd seen her.

Maybe because he understood what it was like to be adopted. He knew about the hurt that caused—no matter how loving the family who'd adopted him had been. There was still a hole left—a hole filled with unanswered questions that lingered in a person's gut.

"Everything okay?" Amberly's suspicious gaze fluttered to each of them as she pulled her arms more tightly around her chest.

"It's fine," Charlie said. "Go back inside."

Amberly stared at her a moment, and Monroe saw the resentment rising in Amberly. Saw the teen's eyes narrow and fill with anger. Saw her shoulders tense. Her breathing become shallower.

She fisted her hands and pounded them at her sides. "Everything is not fine! Everyone here knows that everything isn't fine! But you won't even tell me what's going on. You treat me like I'm a baby."

"Maybe that's because you act like a baby some-times." Charlie raised her chin, not one to handle being disrespected.

"That's not fair!" Amberly let out a half-grunt, half-scream before storming back inside.

Charlie lowered her head and rubbed her temples the way she did when she was unsure if she'd done the right thing.

Monroe didn't see that reaction from her often. But he could identify the burst of self-doubt when-ever it happened—probably because seeing any inse-curity in Charlie was so surprising.

Jesse and Hudson still lingered nearby as well.

Charlie was usually so careful when other people were around.

Charlie started to step toward the door, to go after Amberly, but Monroe held out a hand to block her. "Why don't you let me talk to her?"

"You would do that?" Charlie stared up at him in surprise.

He nodded. "She reminds me a lot of my little sister. I think I can handle it."

"And you're feeling up for the task?"

"I am."

Charlie squeezed his arm. "Thank you."

Gratitude stretched through her voice.

Seeing that reaction would make all this worth it.

Charlie felt the tension in her chest, and she didn't like it.

Sending the cops here tonight had been one more way these people were attacking her.

But she needed to pinpoint exactly who was behind everything. Who was coming after her. Then she could stop them.

Until she did, the attacks would keep coming.

Charlie turned back to Jesse and Hudson, trying to focus her thoughts again.

They all needed to do some damage control.

She needed to talk to her current guests and explain what happened. Certainly, they were all anxious now. She currently had six different women here—four of whom had children with them.

"Our first priority is checking on everyone," she explained. "Gather the staff, and let's split up to talk to our guests and calm them down. Unless you have a personal relationship or connection with the woman, bring a female operative with you. Okay?"

"You got it, Charlie." Jesse tipped his cowboy hat at her.

"We're going to get this figured out," Hudson said.

The two of them scattered. As they did, Charlie started toward the first guest cabin.

Jesse and Hudson could probably tell that she was out of sorts.

And she didn't like that.

Being a female boss had its challenges. The position required a mix of remaining strong and showing just the right amount of softness when necessary.

But if she looked weak, the men under her wouldn't respect her choices. She couldn't allow that to happen.

What happened here tonight felt toxic.

She hadn't come this far to fail.

She had to fix this.

More than anything, she wanted the women here to feel safe.

Right now, that was all on the line.

MONROE KNOCKED on Amberly's door and waited for her to answer.

Finally, she jerked the door open and stared at him with a scowl on her face.

"Hey," he started.

"Hey." She continued to scowl, appearing perturbed that he'd disturbed her.

"We need to talk." He nodded to the couch. "Want to sit?"

"Fine." She stomped across the room and plopped down on the end of the couch, her motions stiff and her bottom lip protruding.

She clearly wasn't happy.

"Everything okay out there?" She finally drew her gaze to meet his, a hint of curiosity in the depths of her eyes.

He lowered himself onto the other end of the couch, a comfortable distance away. "Charlie's handling it."

"She handles everything, doesn't she?" Amberly rolled her eyes.

"Charlie is *really* good at what she does."

"That's what I've been told." She let out a sigh before staring at nothing and giving it a dirty look.

Monroe licked his lips, not wanting to overstep. But he felt as if he had to say something.

"This whole thing has turned Charlie's life upside down also, you know," he started.

Amberly cut her gaze toward him. "I don't feel sorry for her."

"She wouldn't want you to feel sorry for her. That's not what I'm saying. I'm just saying that you should try to put yourself in her shoes also. You're not the only one who's trying to find your footing."

Her bottom lip stuck out farther.

Monroe shifted, deciding to try a different tactic. "You do realize that when you were born, Charlie wasn't much older than you are now."

His pronouncement seemed to send a shockwave of surprise through her. Amberly flinched before shrugging. "I guess . . . I guess I never thought about that."

"The situation wasn't simple." However, Monroe

didn't even know a lot of those details. His curiosity was growing, but Charlie would tell him when she wanted him to know.

"She doesn't even like me," Amberly finally countered.

"That's simply not true." Monroe shifted to fully face her. "Did you know I was adopted?"

Amberly's eyes widened, her full attention now on him. "You were?"

He nodded. "My dad left my mom when I was born, and my mom couldn't handle being a single parent. She comforted herself with drugs until one day she overdosed."

Amberly's eyes widened even more. "Wow. Did you . . . did you find her after she overdosed?"

Monroe nodded, trying not to dive fully into those memories. "I did. I was five at the time, and I didn't have any other family, so I was put into foster care."

"That's a tough place to be."

"You can say that again. I had a couple of really rough homes I lived in until finally, at my fourth foster home, I met my forever family. Rod and Julie Davis. They adopted me and gave me a good life. But I know all about having those feelings of abandonment. They're hard to stomach."

Her gaze flickered up to his. "That's one way to put it."

"But instead of dwelling on the bad stuff that happened, I decided to be grateful for the blessings in it all. Rod and Julie gave me a great life. I'm still close to them to this day. They had four biological children, whom I consider to be my brothers and sisters."

"I'm glad it worked out for you. But who's to say it's gonna work out for me?" She stared at Monroe as she waited for his response.

She appeared to really want the answer—almost as if she feared what her future might hold, like she feared the worst.

Being alone without anyone.

Wasn't that the fear of so many people?

Monroe had even thought about it while he was in the hospital.

Her fears were understandable given the circumstances.

Monroe prayed he'd have the right words.

He shifted and lowered his voice. "This ranch is an incredible place, and your mom is an incredible woman. You just need to give it a chance. I think you could be happy here. I think it could . . . work out."

Amberly puckered out her bottom lip again but didn't deny his words.

Maybe—just maybe—he'd gotten through to her.

He prayed that was the case.

———

Charlie felt her heart lift as she headed home after talking to the women and when she remembered Monroe was at her place.

Usually, she treasured staying alone.

But there was something strangely comforting about knowing someone was there waiting for her.

Of course, Amberly was staying there. But there was so much friction between the two of them that her presence hadn't been a comfort. Charlie didn't think she'd ever be able to break through and reach her daughter.

Instead, Amberly would always blame Charlie for putting her up for adoption. She would never understand that Charlie had been trying to do right by her daughter instead of harming her.

Maybe Charlie had messed up. Maybe she'd made a royal mistake, and she should have kept Amberly.

But deep inside, she knew that wasn't true.

Amberly had been much better off with Patrick and Jamie. The two had been unable to have children on their own. They'd been missionaries living in

Africa for five years before moving back to the States and starting a halfway house for women.

They didn't have a lot of money, but they seemed happy and grounded.

Charlie had known from the moment she met the couple that they would be the perfect fit. They were great examples of living a life of service and selflessness. Their love for each other—and others—had been obvious and so admirable.

Monroe stepped out of the bedroom as soon as Charlie came inside.

He studied her like he always did before asking, "You good?"

Charlie paused near the door and nodded. "About as good as I can be."

She glanced at Amberly's room.

"She's lying down and trying to get some rest," Monroe explained.

Charlie stepped closer to him. "How is she?"

"I think she's going to be okay. She's the type who will need a lot of time to adjust. She doesn't like change."

Charlie let out a biting laugh. She didn't really like change much either.

"It sounds like she talked to you." Her gaze wandered to meet Monroe's. "She didn't shut you out."

"We did talk, and it went well."

"I'm glad. Thank you."

"I really just think the two of you need to find some common ground, that's all."

Charlie let his words sink in. "Maybe you're right. Certainly, there's something that interests us both."

"Just give it some time." Monroe stepped closer. "You look like you've had a rough day."

"That's because I have."

He stepped behind her and gently kneaded the knots in her neck.

Charlie felt herself begin to melt at his touch.

Before she could relish the moment, a jangle pulled her from her thoughts.

Her phone.

Someone was calling about a horse that needed to be rescued.

She stepped away from Monroe's skillful fingers and grabbed a pen and paper from a table near the couch. She quickly jotted down the information.

"Thanks for letting me know about this," she muttered to the caller—a neighbor who wanted to report the horse. "I'll see what I can do."

"Don't wait too long," the man warned. "I don't know how long this horse has."

Charlie frowned. She didn't like to hear that.

She ended the call and lowered her phone into her lap.

"Another horse?" Monroe asked.

"Yes. This one isn't too far away. She's a mustang —" Before Charlie could finish the statement, her phone rang again.

She wanted to ignore it.

But when she saw it was Pierce, she knew she couldn't.

"PIERCE . . . WHAT'S GOING ON?" Charlie's back muscles tensed with anticipation over what he might tell her.

"I thought you'd want to know that I found someone who might know something about the Turleys, but she'll only talk to you."

"She'll only talk to me?" Surprise raced through Charlie.

"That's right. You up for another trip out here?"

"When?"

"Tomorrow morning."

Charlie didn't have to think about it long. She couldn't miss this opportunity. "I'll be there."

"Perfect."

"Wait . . . Pierce." She shifted, her thoughts still racing. "How did you find this person?"

"I'll explain more when you get here. But, just to satisfy some of your curiosity, we discovered that the Turleys have a son—"

"What? Really?" She'd looked into their backgrounds and hadn't seen anything about children.

"The Turleys scrubbed any mention of him from the internet. Their son moved, *and* he changed his name."

Charlie blinked. "That's . . . intriguing."

"I know. It sure is. We found this woman through him. I'll tell you more later."

She ended the call and dropped to the couch. Monroe slowly lowered himself into the seat beside her. "Well?"

She explained the conversation to him.

"So, you're going to go back to Baltimore to meet this woman *and* you're going to rescue a horse and run this ranch and oversee the lodge being built?" He stared at her as he waited for her response.

He was clearly anxious about everything Charlie was trying to handle.

She pressed her eyes closed at the reminder of her responsibilities. "That's what I've been doing."

He squeezed her arm. "You can't do all of this on your own."

"I don't. I have people who work for me—"

"But you do the majority of the workload here on

your own," Monroe gently reminded her. "You might want to take some things off your plate."

"I'm too much of a control freak to do that."

"Maybe . . . but that can change."

Charlie turned toward him, emotion suddenly flooding her. "How could I possibly hand this off to someone else?"

"Take baby steps. Start with getting an assistant who can handle the details."

She frowned. "Have I mentioned that I have trust issues?"

"What about Sarah Chamberlain?" He stared at her as he waited for her reaction.

"Sarah?" Charlie had never considered her.

Sarah was dating one of Charlie's operatives, Ruger Stark, and Charlie knew the two wanted to live closer together. Sarah was currently in Montana.

"I know she wants to move nearer to Ruger," Monroe continued. "She's a nurse by trade, and it would be handy to have a medical professional here at all times instead of having to call Dr. Cossette in during emergencies."

"That's true . . ."

"And you know you can trust Sarah."

"I do." Maybe the idea was worth considering. But Charlie didn't like making quick decisions.

"If you keep going at this rate, it's going to be detrimental to your health."

She did a double take at him. "Aren't you full of sunshine today?"

He leaned closer. "I'm just worried about you."

"Well, I appreciate that. It's good to have someone worry about me."

"Will you consider my idea, at least?"

She stared into his hazel eyes and nodded. "I will. But only if *you* promise to get some rest. I'm not the only one running on empty here."

A frown tugged at his lips. "I really hate the fact I'm making you sleep on the couch."

"You're not making me do anything." She grabbed a pillow from beside her and gently flung it at him. "I'll be fine. I promise. But I'll sleep a lot better if I know you're okay and healthy."

He stared at her a moment before conceding. "Okay. I understand."

He rose to his feet and stared down at her, an unreadable look in his eyes.

Something unseen passed between them, and tension crackled in the air.

Charlie licked her lips as she remembered the moment they'd shared yesterday.

Was Monroe remembering their almost kiss like she was? Did he long for more as well?

Or was the moment forgotten?

She wasn't sure.

He stepped back. "Good night, Charlie."

"Good night, Monroe." Charlie's throat burned as she said the words . . . especially when she realized how much she wanted to throw her arms around him and take their relationship to the next level.

She hadn't felt that way in a long, long time.

And that fact terrified her.

———

Charlie felt the knots in her back as she landed in Baltimore . . . again.

How many times would she have to take this trip?

As many as it took, she supposed.

She hated to leave the ranch with everything going on. But she couldn't miss the opportunity to find answers. It was what she'd dedicated her life to for years.

The good news was that she should be able to fly back home tonight. It would make for a long day, but whining about it wouldn't help. She just had to push through and get it done.

Her thoughts drifted as her plane taxied down the runway.

Charlie had awakened Monroe this morning to tell him goodbye. His color looked better, which made her feel hopeful that his recovery was progressing as it should.

When Charlie had told Amberly goodbye, her daughter had barely looked at her. Instead, she grunted something before turning over in bed and pulling the covers up higher.

Vanessa should be tutoring her by now, and Charlie hoped Amberly didn't give the woman a hard time again. She also prayed that Amberly and Jonathan stayed away from each other.

She wished she could be there monitoring everything.

Maybe soon she would be able to stay home.

"How's Chesney doing?" Charlie asked Ghost after they were safely in the air.

Chesney was Ghost's girlfriend—an actress.

"She's doing great. About to make a new movie that she's really excited about."

"I'm glad to hear that. You pop the question yet?"

He grinned and cast her a quick glance. "Not yet. But soon."

"Don't let her get away. She's a good one." Not only was Chesney an accomplished actress, but the woman was also kind and generous. She'd become a major supporter of Vanishing Ranch, and she truly believed in their mission.

"Yes, she is." Ghost grinned.

Charlie lapsed into silence for the remainder of the flight.

She might even have dozed off. It didn't seem long before the plane landed, bouncing along the runway until coming to a stop.

The crew outside began to secure it as Charlie watched out the window beside her.

A few minutes later, Ghost cleared her to deplane.

Charlie stood and grabbed her purse. "Thank you again."

He grinned. "No problem, Charlie."

As the door opened, she climbed down the steps. She'd left Arizona at seven a.m. With the time change, it was now one p.m. here on the East Coast.

However, she'd gain time on her flight back later today, so it would all even out.

She scanned the small airport until she spotted the black SUV waiting for her in the parking lot.

Pierce should be waiting inside the vehicle.

She glanced at her watch.

She had only forty minutes to go until she met this mystery woman.

Charlie hoped this trip here was worth it.

"WOW, those bruises on your face still look awful."

Charlie resisted a scowl at Pierce's comment. She'd tried to cover them with makeup, just so people wouldn't ask questions.

Apparently, her makeup tricks hadn't worked.

"What can I say?" Charlie shrugged. "When I do something, I do it right."

"That sounds like you." He turned his eyes back to the parking lot as they headed from the small airport. "You doing okay?"

"As well as can be expected. Anything new that I should know about? How'd you find this lady?" Charlie couldn't wait to learn more details. She didn't like being kept in the dark.

He let out a sigh and stared at the road ahead. "I was digging into the Turleys' past, and I discovered they had a son—I mentioned that to you on the phone."

"You did, but I still don't understand how that's possible."

"Well, when a man and a woman really love each other—"

"Ha ha. I should have known that was coming." Charlie rolled her eyes. "I just don't understand how you were able to track him down."

"It wasn't easy to find this guy. But, of course, I was able to because I had access to his official birth record. Apparently, he was eighteen when the Overland Hotel was bombed. About a year later, his parents supposedly found that lead on the bombing and began to investigate."

"Right." Charlie had an inkling as to where this might be going.

"About the same time they dropped their story, their son—Robert is his name—disappeared."

"Did someone abduct him?" Her mind raced.

"No, his parents gave him a good sum of their savings and sent him to start a new life with a new name."

Realization rolled over Charlie. "Wait . . . someone must have been threatening them. Maybe they were worried that he'd be hurt if they didn't back off."

Pierce glanced at her and grinned. "Exactly."

"Did he know anything about what happened?"

"Not much. He said his parents didn't like to talk about it. But they did leave him a jump drive. They said only to open it in the event of their deaths."

Her heart thrummed harder. "Did he give it to you?"

"He did. There was only one thing on it. The name Suzy Mercer."

She sucked in a breath. "The woman we're going to talk to . . ."

"It wasn't easy to find her. Not at all. But I happened to show her picture to a colleague, and he said he'd seen her a couple of times while out on patrol. She's in the drug scene. That brings us to today."

The drug scene? How reliable would she be?

"To today," Charlie repeated as she processed this new information.

"Any idea why this woman won't talk to anyone but you?" Pierce glanced at her as they continued down the busy road.

"Your guess is as good as mine. Maybe name recognition?"

He narrowed his eyes as if he didn't buy that theory.

"Do you have another idea?" Charlie asked.

He shrugged, and his grip on the steering wheel tightened. "Not really. But I know you're not telling me everything, so I'm proceeding with caution."

She didn't apologize for keeping certain details to herself. She had her own reasons for doing that, and she didn't need to explain.

Twenty minutes later, they pulled to a stop at an outdated motel in a seedy part of town.

Charlie stared at the building. "This is where we're meeting?"

Her gut told her this place could be trouble.

"This is the address the woman gave me," Pierce said. "Do you want to turn around and leave?"

Charlie opened the SUV door. She hadn't come this far to back down.

"No way," she murmured. "Let's go see what this woman has to say."

———

Monroe stepped outside of Charlie's place, needing some fresh air.

He had several things on his agenda for today. But he hadn't mentioned any of them to Charlie. He knew she would have insisted he rest.

As he sucked in a deep breath of cool desert air, his thoughts wandered.

Pierce . . . Charlie had said his name during that phone conversation. But who was Pierce? Was he Amberly's father? And why hadn't Charlie ever mentioned him before?

The questions circled in his head.

Maybe he would ask Charlie one day.

Maybe not.

When it came to Charlie, he didn't like to push for answers. She was the type who said what she needed to say when she was ready to share it.

As he started toward the mess hall, Hudson fell into step beside him.

"How are you feeling?" Hudson asked.

Monroe couldn't help but wonder if Charlie had told the staff here to watch out for him. It wouldn't surprise him.

"Been better, been worse," he finally answered.

Hudson nodded. "I get that. You gave us all a good scare."

"I'm sure I did. I'm halfway glad I can't remember everything that went down."

"That's probably a blessing." They paused by the doors to the main building, and Hudson turned toward him. "For what it's worth, I thought I'd let you know that I've never seen Charlie like she was after that grenade was thrown."

Monroe felt himself go still as he turned to Hudson. "What do you mean?"

Hudson glanced in the distance before his gaze connected with Monroe's again. "Charlie is always so calm and in control, never showing any signs that she could break. Until the grenade. I practically had to pull her off you so paramedics could take you away."

Monroe's heart pounded harder.

Charlie had been that concerned?

In a strange way, knowing that touched him.

Hudson clamped a hand around Monroe's bicep. "Either way, we're glad you're back now."

He snapped from his thoughts. "Glad to be back."

"Let's do a campfire sometime soon. We miss hearing you sing with your guitar around here."

"Sounds like a plan." Monroe missed those simple times as well.

He wandered into the mess hall, said hello to several people, then went into his office.

He sat behind his desk, marveling at the fact that he was back.

Things had been touch-and-go there for a while.

He saw Jesse passing and called to him. The operative paused in the doorway.

"The residents here doing okay this morning?" Monroe asked.

Jesse nodded and took a sip of coffee. "They seem to be. I know Charlie isn't here, but we've been trying to figure out a plan just in case the cops come back."

"They *will* come back." Monroe's jaw hardened. "It's just a matter of when. Did you guys come up with anything?"

Jesse frowned and shook his head. "Not yet. We thought about taking the women and children to the lodge. If the cops get a warrant to search this place, the lodge shouldn't be included in the search parameters."

Monroe twisted his head skeptically. "But the women won't feel safe there . . ."

Jesse's frown deepened. "We thought of that also, but we aren't sure what to do about that."

"Let's keep brainstorming. We'll meet with Charlie when she gets back." Monroe shifted. "What about this Detective Vincent? Did you find out anything about him?"

Jesse stepped into the office and sat down in the chair across from him, settling in for what would obviously be a longer conversation. "As a matter of fact, I did. Detective Vincent has apparently only been a part of the ASPC for the past three months. He moved here from Virginia."

"What part?"

"Near DC."

Monroe grunted. That didn't surprise him.

He had a feeling DC politics were deeply intertwined with the corruption he and Charlie were investigating.

"What's his record like?" Monroe shifted as his shoulder began to ache.

"Surprisingly clean. I mean, even the best cops have a few things on their record that could look suspicious."

"But his record looks as if it's been wiped?" Monroe finished.

"Bingo." Jesse gave him a look.

Apprehension churned inside Monroe.

He didn't like where this was going.

Because he could feel the walls closing in—and fast.

CHARLIE AND PIERCE paused by room 208 and stared at the pink door for only a moment before knocking.

Beside her, the curtain fluttered—though just barely.

Still, no one answered.

Charlie glanced around as she waited, making sure trouble wasn't anywhere close.

She saw nothing that raised her suspicions.

She knocked again.

Finally, the door cracked open, the safety chain stretched across the small opening.

She couldn't tell much about the person staring back at her. Only that it was a woman with pale skin who, if Charlie had to guess, was close to her own age.

"Charlie?" Her voice came out at a croak.

"It's me. You said you wanted to meet."

Her gaze went to Pierce then back to Charlie. "Just you."

Charlie turned to Pierce and gave him a look.

He narrowed his eyes as if annoyed. "I'll wait out here."

Charlie wouldn't argue with him about that.

Finally, Suzy Mercer opened the door. The woman was incredibly thin with stringy blonde hair and patchy skin.

Charlie didn't want to jump to conclusions, but she'd guess the woman was on drugs. She'd seen the look before.

Charlie stepped inside the old hotel room.

The place had two double beds with brown and orange comforters on them. A strange scent filled the air —maybe body odor mixed with cheap air freshener and trash that needed to be taken out. Clothes and other items were strewn over every surface and the floor.

Clearly, housekeeping hadn't been inside in a while.

The woman rubbed her hands on her mint-green jeans and pointed at the bed. "I know it's not much but have a seat."

Charlie pushed some clothes out of the way

before lowering herself on the edge of the bed nearest the door. The woman sat across from her on the other.

"I understand that you wanted to talk to me," Charlie started, as she noted the woman's trembling hands.

"That's right. Thank you for coming." Her gaze nervously darted about.

Silence stretched a moment, the only sound the heat clicking on and noisily blaring warm air into the room.

Charlie shifted on the bed. "So what exactly did you want to talk to me about?"

Suzy's gaze met hers. "I know what happened during the bombing at the Overland Hotel. But anyone I've ever told has ended up dead."

———

Charlie's breath caught.

The Overland Hotel.

Suzy claimed to have information—information that had gotten other people killed.

"What do you know, Suzy?" Charlie tried to keep her voice firm but gentle. She needed to conceal the urgency and desperation she felt.

The woman was skittish, and Charlie didn't want to scare her off.

Suzy stared at her hands as they rested in her lap. "When I was thirteen years old, I got mad at my dad and ran away from home. My first night sleeping in a bus station, I met a guy who said he could take care of me. I thought God had sent him to me and that he was an answer to my prayers. At first, he did take care of me. He was fantastic, and I fell totally and completely in love."

The story sounded familiar. She'd heard it many times.

Charlie waited for her to continue.

Suzy sniffled as if trying to hold herself together and find the courage to finish. "Then he started asking me to do things I didn't want to do. When I told him no, he got rough with me. That's when I realized he was no angel. I tried to get away, but I couldn't. I had no money, nowhere to go, and no one to depend on. I felt so . . . trapped."

Charlie had heard similar tales more times than she wanted to count. If the circumstances in Charlie's own life had taken a different path, she might have found herself in this woman's shoes.

She was so thankful Greta had stepped in to help her.

Suzy kept her gaze averted and continued, almost

as if the pain from telling this story was unbearable. "Fast forward six months, and I was being sold to the highest bidder."

Charlie's heart panged with grief at her words. "I'm so sorry."

Suzy's gaze fluttered up, and she nodded before looking away again. "I know some women escape from human trafficking and walk away stronger. Not me. I've been messed up ever since."

"But you escaped?"

"I'll get to that part of the story in a moment. The truth is my so-called boyfriend, Eric, had some pretty big connections. He traveled in some noteworthy circles. I didn't know who exactly was in those circles at the time. Everything was hush-hush. But I know pictures and photos were taken."

"To blackmail the people involved," Charlie finished.

Suzy nodded. "Yes, I found out later that was why. They were in 'compromising' positions, and their sins could be leveraged for favors if others kept quiet."

Maybe this woman really did have some of the answers Charlie had been desperately searching for.

Charlie shifted as something bubbled inside her.

Excitement? Anticipation? Apprehension?

Maybe it was all three.

"ONE DAY, Eric was transporting me to a new location." Suzy swallowed hard as she slumped on the edge of the bed. "As he transferred me from one van to another, I looked up and saw my father staring at me from across the street. My mom died when I was young, so it was just Dad and me for the longest time. We were always really close—until we had that fight over my clothing and friend choices. But, right then, I felt so much hope. Almost just as quickly, I realized how ashamed he must be of me."

Charlie gave the woman a moment to compose herself. Suzy's breath was shallow, her limbs trembled, and her eyes appeared almost glassy.

This clearly wasn't easy for her.

"I tried to hide my face." Suzy rubbed her cheek, almost frantically. "But my dad had already seen me.

He ran across the street and confronted Eric. There was a big fight, but then the police came around the corner, and Eric saw them, so he ran. My dad saved me."

"Talk about great timing," Charlie said.

A tear rolled down Suzy's cheek. "Absolutely. I just knew I'd finally be free. My dad took me home, and I went to the hospital to be checked out. I filed a report with the FBI and went through therapy. What I didn't realize was the toll this all had taken on my dad."

"I can only imagine."

Suzy dragged her gaze up to meet Charlie's. "When Eric had me under his control, one of the places he would take me was the Overland Hotel down in Florida."

Charlie's breath caught at her words. "Is that right?"

"The other girls and I would sit in the lobby, dressed to the nines. We would sip our drinks and talk and try to look sophisticated. It wasn't that we wanted to be there. But the control these men had over us . . ."

"I understand." Charlie squeezed her arm. "You were living under so much fear that running didn't seem like a choice. They're good at manipulating women that way."

Relief seemed to fill Suzy, grateful that Charlie understood.

She continued. "This particular hotel had an atrium in the middle, and all the rooms surrounded it. Guests could step out of their rooms, look down from their balconies, and see everyone in the dining area."

Charlie nodded. She was familiar with hotels with that layout.

"The men would then pick which one of us they wanted. We all wore different colors, so we'd be easier to distinguish. Then we'd casually walk to the rooms to meet with our 'clients.'"

"That sounds horrific. I'm so sorry."

Suzy nodded, though barely. "It was. After I was rescued, my dad heard a big conference was going to be held there, and he saw his opportunity to confront some of the men who'd hurt me."

Charlie's heart pounded faster as she anticipated where this might be going. "Was he able to do that?"

Suzy rubbed her throat. "He did. There in the hotel. Security broke up the fight, but he said that this wouldn't be the end of it. But then . . ."

"The explosion killed everyone inside," Charlie said.

Suzy nodded. "My dad had already been kicked out for causing a disruption. But he always knew there was more to that explosion, that it wasn't a terrorist attack."

Charlie's hopes soared. Her dad must have seen or heard something to make him suspicious.

"Can I talk to your dad?" Charlie asked.

"No." Another tear rolled down Suzy's cheek. "He was killed in a car accident two days later."

Charlie's heart throbbed in her ears. "But it wasn't an accident, was it?"

Suzy shook her head. "I know it wasn't. But no one else believed me . . . except for one person."

"Who was that?"

She shifted, dragging her gaze up to meet Charlie's. "Your dad."

"What?" Certainly, Charlie hadn't heard correctly.

Suzy nodded. "I knew his mom had died in the explosion. I knew he was going to war to fight these guys who supposedly caused it."

"How did you find him to talk to him?" It wasn't as if her father was easily accessible—especially when he'd been stationed overseas.

"The day before he left for his mission, I heard he was doing a press conference. It was nearby. I knew it was a longshot, but I went. I stayed in the shadows so no one would see me. Then, before he climbed into his car to leave, I called his name. I didn't think he'd heard me at first, but he did."

"And?" Charlie's heart thumped harder as she waited to hear the rest of the story.

"I told him I knew something about his mom's death that I needed to tell him. He asked me to meet him at a restaurant down the street. There were too many people around to talk right there. So I went there. He came in looking as if he were undercover. He wore a hat and sunglasses. I guess he still had a lot of fans who liked to follow his every move."

"That sounds about right."

"He bought me dinner and listened to my story. I wasn't sure how he'd react. I feared he might think I was crazy." Suzy paused. "Instead, he thanked me for being brave and coming forward. Then he told me he'd look into it. Before he left, he gave me some money so I could get back on my feet."

"And then?"

"He left for war. I heard he died two months later."

Charlie reeled.

Had her dad taken Suzy's words to heart? Had he started asking questions?

Was that what had ultimately gotten him killed?

Charlie knew the answer.

Yes. A resounding yes.

But why hadn't they killed Suzy too?

Charlie knew her time was limited, so she pushed

ahead with the rest of her questions. "What happened to you afterward?"

"I went into hiding. Tried to make sure those men never found me. I'd hoped they would eventually stop looking. That maybe they thought I was a nobody. That no one of consequence would ever take me seriously. But sometimes I still feel as if I'm being watched. Like if I make one wrong move, I'll have some type of tragic accident also."

Charlie shifted, one predominant question pressing on her. "Suzy . . . do you know the names of any of those men who hurt you?"

She glanced up, and her gaze connected with Charlie's. "I didn't know at the time. But I do now."

———

Charlie's thoughts wouldn't stop racing through all the horrific details Suzy had just shared.

Charlie had always admired her dad. But now she thought she admired him even more.

She swallowed hard as she tucked those thoughts away.

Her gaze locked with Suzy's. "Suzy, can you tell me who those men are?"

"I can. But I need your help getting out of here

first." Her gaze wavered as if she was trying to hold it steady but couldn't quite do it.

"Out of this hotel?" Charlie wasn't sure she'd understood her correctly.

She nodded. "You don't understand. I've been on the run for the past fifteen years. Taking on jobs here and there and staying at hotels. Sometimes on the streets."

"Because you were afraid these guys would find you," Charlie finished.

"Yes. Fear has consumed me every day. I knew I couldn't go back home, that they would track me there."

"What kind of jobs have you been working?"

Shame filled her gaze. "Just this and that."

Charlie thought she knew what that meant.

Suzy had been doing the one thing she'd been taught made her worthwhile, hadn't she? Selling herself for sex.

Compassion filled Charlie.

"Why did you ask for me?" Charlie needed to make sure she had all these puzzle pieces in place before she made any recommendations on how she could help.

Because there was still a lot she didn't know.

Charlie liked to vet the people she helped. The last thing she needed was to attempt to help someone who secretly wanted to bring her down and reveal her secrets.

Unfortunately, that was the world she lived in. It wasn't pretty, but those facts were reality.

"That detective called me and told me my name had been found in a file those reporters had left. I thought this might be my chance. I've been wanting to talk to you for years. I just didn't know how to get in touch. Whenever I heard you were doing speaking engagements, they were too far away for me to travel. So I decided to leverage the detective's request."

"Smart thinking." Charlie remained silent several moments until she finally nodded. "Okay. Why don't you grab a few things. I'll get you out of here and take you somewhere safe."

Suzy's fidgeting stopped for a moment as their gazes locked. "You promise?"

Charlie nodded. "I know just the place."

CHAPTER
NINETEEN

"YOU'RE TAKING her back to your horse farm?" Pierce stared at Charlie as if she'd lost her mind.

But that didn't deter her. "Suzy needs somewhere safe to go."

He glanced at the hotel door behind them as they stood outside and spoke in hushed tones while Suzy packed her things.

"I should talk to her first." Pierce shifted as if trying to recalculate.

"She has nothing to say pertaining to your case."

He dropped his head to the side, irritation in his gaze. "Come on, Charlie. Don't act like I'm dumb."

"I know you're not dumb." She tried to soften her approach. "But this goes back to my father."

"How did this woman know I was connected with you?"

"She's been waiting for the right opportunity to talk to me. She saw this as an opening."

Pierce continued to eye her. "It has nothing to do with Margaret or the Turleys' deaths?"

"That's right." Charlie kept her gaze level, not wanting him to know the entire truth of the situation. Not yet, at least. "I'm sorry that you got pulled into the middle of this."

Pierce stepped closer and lowered his voice. "I know there's more to the story, Charlie."

"I can't tell you the details. If they affected you, I would. But they don't. Please believe me."

"It's hard to believe you when you're keeping me in the dark. Then again, maybe that's par for the course."

Charlie bristled. "That's not fair."

"But it is, isn't it?"

Tension pulled across her chest. "I don't really want to get into this now."

"I'm sure you don't."

More irritation pinched at her nerves.

"I've already explained the truth," Charlie said in a low tone. "Many times. And you still choose not to believe me."

Instead of dwelling on this conversation, Charlie scanned the parking lot. Her gaze stopped on a man lingering across the street.

"Who is that?" She nodded at him. "One of your guys?"

Pierce followed her gaze. "He's been there a while. Waiting for the bus. Nothing suspicious about that. But no. He's not with me."

"No buses have been by in the last few minutes then?"

"Just one, but you know they don't all go to the same places, right? He could be waiting for a different one."

"I'm aware." Charlie tried to keep the irritation from her voice but was unsuccessful.

Instead, she continued to stare at the man. He wore a black puffer style coat and a matching knit hat. Even though he wore sunglasses, Charlie sensed he was watching her. It was almost as if he looked too casual.

"Charlie . . . I think you're reading too much into this." Warning edged Pierce's voice.

She ignored it. "Stay here and watch Suzy's room."

She didn't wait for Pierce to answer before she started toward the steps.

"Charlie . . . you're not going after him." Pierce stepped behind her.

"I just want to have a conversation."

"Charlie . . ."

But she wouldn't be deterred.

As soon as Charlie reached the stairs, she hurried down and across the parking lot. She started toward the street so she could cross it near the bus stop.

As she did, the man looked up and his eyes widened.

Was that recognition in his gaze?

Yes, it was.

"Hey! Wait one minute." She sensed he was about to run.

And she was right.

Because before she could even get across the street, he darted away.

———

Charlie reached the other side of the street and sprinted toward the man.

But he had a decent head start and was faster than she'd anticipated.

He cut behind a laundromat, down a narrow alleyway.

Charlie paused in front of the corridor and scanned the space.

She was desperate for answers, but she wasn't stupid.

She made a note of where the alley ended—there were two possible directions.

Then she continued down the main street and took the next right.

She ran down the sidewalk, ignoring the people who stared at her and some of the lewd comments muttered by those lingering on the streets.

She paused where the alley should have spilled out.

No one was there.

This man hadn't disappeared into thin air. So where had he gone?

Charlie glanced around one more time, looking for any sign of him.

As she did, a car in the distance roared to life. The next second, it squealed into the street—headed right toward her.

TWENTY

CHARLIE DOVE out of the way, her hip colliding with the sidewalk as she landed hard then rolled.

The car swerved away, only inches from hitting her.

Her heart pounded as she rose and wiped off her jeans.

She tried to see the license plate, but she couldn't make it out.

The car was too far away.

She sighed and headed back toward Pierce. She wasn't in the mood to hear his scolding.

"What were you thinking?" he demanded as soon as she reached the hotel.

Apparently, he must have heard the commotion.

"I was thinking this isn't the time to just stand back and do nothing. That maybe I could find answers. If I want to know something, then I need to go for it. I can't miss an opportunity."

He scowled. "You've always taken a little too much initiative—more than is good for you. One day that's not going to work in your favor."

She ignored his remark and glanced at her watch, an uneasy feeling in her stomach.

Someone knew she was here and had followed her.

That could mean other people—dangerous people were nearby also.

"I haven't seen anyone else," Pierce said as if reading her mind.

Charlie glanced at the motel door, noting that Suzy still wasn't out. "I need to get to the airport. The longer I stay here with her, the more danger we're going to be in."

Pierce's eyebrows flickered. "Sounds like this woman has some pretty nasty guys after her."

"Let's just say she's been hiding for a long time, and there are people who have very good reasons for wanting her dead."

Pierce gave her another look. "I don't like the sound of that."

"You aren't supposed to like the sound of that."

"Just saying."

The pink door behind them opened, and Suzy

stood there. She'd put on a hat and an oversized jacket as if hoping it would disguise her. She nervously glanced back and forth between Charlie and Pierce.

"You ready to go?" Charlie asked.

Suzy hefted a small book bag on her shoulders and nodded.

Glancing around protectively once more, Charlie led her to Pierce's SUV and tucked her in the backseat. She prayed they'd get to the airport in one piece.

———

Monroe had a hard time sitting still.

He'd already walked around the ranch several times.

The doctor had said it was important that he move and not just sit around all day.

But now he needed something to keep his mind occupied.

It seemed he had plenty.

He'd texted Charlie earlier and asked if the police had identified the man who'd attacked her inside Margaret Creighton's place. Several minutes later, Charlie had gotten back to him with a name.

Angelo Martinez.

Monroe went to his office again and hopped on his computer to see what he could find out about the man.

The guy was a thirty-four-year-old construction worker with no prior record.

So why had he gone to that house? What had he been trying to accomplish?

Local police painted the incident as a break-in, but Monroe didn't believe that. Anyone who knew the details about Margaret and the Turleys wouldn't.

So maybe someone had hired this guy. Or maybe they'd manipulated him into doing the job.

Monroe nodded.

Manipulation made more sense to him.

So what had someone been holding over him?

Monroe typed a few more things into his computer until he found his answer.

Angelo had an eight-year-old daughter named Gia. Angelo had split from the girl's mom, and now his daughter and his ex lived in West Virginia—quite a drive from Baltimore.

Someone needed to talk to them. Monroe would bet Angelo's daughter had been threatened and used as leverage. That the man had been coerced into that break-in.

And he'd died rather than face the consequences of his daughter being harmed.

Monroe did a quick internet search until he found the mother's number.

He called her.

The phone rang and rang until he was certain no one would pick up.

Then, on the sixth ring, a man answered.

"Annetta?" he rushed.

"I'm sorry . . . this isn't Annetta. In fact, I was trying to reach her."

"Who are you?" the man demanded.

"I'm just someone looking for answers."

"Well, she's not here. I don't know where she is!"

Before Monroe could ask any more questions, the call ended.

Annetta and her daughter were in trouble, weren't they?

Monroe had to let someone know.

TWENTY-ONE

THANKFULLY, Charlie and Suzy arrived at the airport without issue.

Ghost and his copilot waited on the private jet to take them back to Arizona.

Charlie was ready to be gone from Baltimore. She was ready to be back home with Monroe and Amberly.

Pierce escorted her and Suzy to the stairway.

"I'll be right there," Charlie told Suzy. She watched as the woman disappeared into the plane before turning to Pierce. "Thank you for everything."

"If there's anything I need to know . . ." Suspicion still edged his voice.

"I'll be in touch."

As she turned to go, Pierce grabbed her arm. "Charlie, if you're in trouble . . . I can help you."

That wasn't what he'd told her fifteen years ago.

Charlie wanted to pull herself from his grasp, but she didn't. "I appreciate that. But I'm fine."

She tried to step away again, but he still held on.

Now she was getting irritated.

His gaze locked on hers. "What have you gotten yourself caught up in the middle of?"

"A real-life conspiracy," Charlie admitted to him. "If I told you, someone would try to kill you."

"You don't think I'm a target already?"

She raised an eyebrow. "Are you?"

"I've noticed two men in black suits following me around ever since we went to the Turleys' house."

Her breath caught. "You have? You didn't mention that to me."

"I'm not sure it's related. I work a lot of cases, in case you didn't know that."

Of course, Charlie knew that. Didn't all detectives have full caseloads?

"Then you need to watch your step," she finally said.

"I always do." Pierce stepped closer. "We could work together on this, you know."

Her throat tightened at the thought of it. "That's not a good idea. I work alone."

He stared her down another moment before

letting out a soft chuckle. "You always were the rebellious type."

"If you say so."

His gaze softened as he observed her. "You know, I thought we were good together."

This was *not* where she wanted this conversation to go. "We weren't. You have a selective memory."

He chuckled again. "I assure you, I don't. I remember everything."

She leveled her gaze with him. "So do I."

"Are you still holding it against me that—"

"The past is the past," Charlie rushed, not wanting to get into this here. "Now, I've got to go. I have an appointment I need to be back for tonight."

Pierce released her arm and stepped back. "Okay then. But I have a feeling we're going to be in touch again soon."

Charlie hoped that wasn't the case.

She was ready for all this to be over.

———

As Charlie and Suzy got settled on the plane, Charlie tried to force her shoulders to relax.

It wasn't quite that easy.

Her thoughts raced too much as she reviewed everything she'd learned.

She and Suzy still had a lot to talk about, but they would wait until the plane was airborne to start.

They had a four-hour flight to chat.

Ghost did his preflight check with them, and they pulled on their seatbelts.

A moment later, the jet began to taxi toward the runway.

The engine revved as the line of pavement stretched before them.

"I always get so nervous before takeoff," Suzy muttered as she nearly choked the armrest beside her.

Charlie squeezed her arm. "I know. A lot of people do. But don't worry—Ghost is one of the best. He'll get us in the air safely."

Suzy nodded but still looked unconvinced.

A moment later, they began to race down the runway.

Charlie squeezed Suzy's hand again, trying to comfort her.

Then she heard Ghost mutter, "Uh-oh."

Charlie's lungs froze. Uh-oh?

She didn't think she'd ever heard Ghost say that before.

She leaned toward the cockpit, trying to figure out what he was talking about.

That's when she saw two SUVs on the runway, stopped directly in their path.

"WHAT'S GOING ON?" Suzy rushed, her gaze darting around the cabin.

Charlie forced herself to take several deep breaths and swallow her panic. "Just hold tight."

Suzy glanced out the window—but from her angle, the cars remained out of sight. "Are we going to crash or something?"

"We should be fine." Charlie's heart pounded in her ears.

"Then why did he say uh-oh?"

"Just a minor hiccup." Charlie prayed that was the case.

She peered out the front window again, her gaze fixated on those SUVs blocking them.

Someone didn't want them taking off.

Most likely the same person who'd been watching her earlier.

The person who didn't want Suzy spilling everything she knew.

Ghost muttered something indecipherable to his copilot.

The plane continued to race forward.

Shouldn't they stop instead?

But stopping would just ensure these men could board the plane.

They couldn't let that happen.

But continuing forward . . . that could get them all killed.

Charlie's eyes remained open—unable to close them or look away—but she began lifting frantic prayers for their safety.

Meanwhile, they got closer and closer to the SUVs.

How would Ghost avoid hitting them?

The plane couldn't take off after that kind of damage.

"Charlie . . ." Suzy muttered beside her.

"I know." Tension spread through Charlie's chest.

Finally, Charlie pressed her eyes closed.

At any moment, they would slam into those vehicles.

Would there be an explosion?

Would death come instantly?

Or would they be left alive with life-altering burns and injuries?

The questions rushed through her mind.

Nothing happened.

Not yet.

It was taking longer than Charlie thought to hit the vehicles.

The wheels no longer rumbled along the runway.

The plane ride had become smooth.

Almost like . . .

Finally, she plucked an eye open.

She released her breath.

They were airborne! How had that . . . ?

"Ghost?" she muttered.

"That was a close one," he called over his shoulder.

She leaned across the seat and looked out the window across the aisle.

Sure enough, the vehicles were now behind them.

Four men in black stared at them, talking animatedly.

She released the rest of her breath she'd kept frozen in her lungs.

She and Suzy were safe . . . for now.

But Charlie had no doubt these guys would keep coming after them.

———

Once the plane reached a safe altitude, Charlie had grabbed Suzy some water and a sandwich from what was stocked on the plane.

Then she turned toward the woman, knowing they didn't have time to waste.

These guys were hot on their trail and determined to stop Charlie from finding out any of these answers.

If men were desperate enough to bomb a hotel in the middle of a convention to kill innocent people in order to keep their silence, then these men wouldn't hesitate to kill Charlie also.

Wouldn't hesitate to destroy her entire ranch—and everyone in it—for that matter.

A hot ball of anger formed inside her at the thought.

"I know that you probably need some time to regroup, but we don't have any time, unfortunately," Charlie said. "You saw what just happened."

Suzy nodded and took a big sip of her water between bites of the sandwich. "It's not easy to talk about."

"I know," Charlie said. "But whoever hurt you needs to be brought down."

She released a long breath before nodding again. "You have a pen and paper?"

Charlie reached into her bag and pulled a legal pad and pen out. "I do."

Then Suzy began naming off a list of people—A-listers.

Politicians. Actors. Business leaders. Doctors.

All people who'd been involved in the Epstein-like crime ring.

All people who had a lot to lose if word got out about them.

Thinking about it made Charlie sick to her stomach.

When Suzy finished, Charlie turned toward her.

There was one name she'd expected to hear but hadn't.

"Did Bill Radar's name ever come up?" she asked.

Suzy frowned and picked at her chicken salad sandwich. She hadn't even eaten half of it yet. "He was never one of my clients. I did hear another girl mention him, though."

"Mention him as a client?"

Suzy shrugged. "It was vague, so I can't say for sure. But I don't think he was the guy in charge."

Charlie practically held her breath. "Do you know who was?"

Suzy frowned and placed her sandwich back on the tray. "I wish I could tell you. But whoever it is, he guards his identity. That makes me think he was someone very powerful."

"More powerful than a former president?"

She shrugged again. "Maybe."

Charlie didn't know who that person was. But if Suzy agreed to it, Charlie knew someone who could take an official statement from her. This was bigger than Vanishing Ranch or any local law enforcement agency.

She might finally have the evidence she needed to push her case forward and get it in front of the right people.

CHAPTER
TWENTY-THREE

MONROE FELT a flash of relief when he saw the helicopter in the distance. He waited outside Charlie's place as it landed.

He would walk out there to meet her, but he knew the gesture probably wouldn't be appreciated. And it was a long way to walk without anywhere to sit down. He hated to admit it, but he still had some healing to do.

He watched as Charlie climbed out.

Then as she waited.

Who was she waiting for?

A moment later, a woman with long blonde hair and a thin build stepped out.

His curiosity grew.

As they walked toward the mess hall, Charlie looked up and their gazes connected.

Silent communication passed between them.

There was more to this story.

Jesse and Hudson met up with them, along with Sienna, Jesse's wife and another Vanishing Ranch operative.

"Sienna," Charlie started. "This is Suzy. I need you to take her to the clinic for me. I'm going to call the doctor to have her checked out, just as a precaution. While Sienna does that, Jesse, I need you to talk to Chef and ask him to make Suzy something good and hearty to eat. Hudson, scrounge up some clothes so she'll have something fresh to wear while we wash what she brought with her. Meanwhile, I'll also need you to talk to Kota so we can get one of the guest cabins ready. Everything make sense?"

Everyone around her nodded.

Charlie turned back to the woman and placed a hand on her arm. "My team here is going to take good care of you. I'm going to let you get rested, but I'll check in with you later, okay?"

The woman, who was probably Charlie's age, looked almost like a child with her frightened eyes. She nodded before walking away with Sienna.

Monroe and Charlie paused in front of each other near the horse pasture.

"How are you feeling?" She studied his face.

"I'm trying to stretch my legs and follow the doctor's orders."

She patted his bicep. "Good boy."

"Why do I have a feeling that you have a lot more to tell me than I have to tell you?"

"Because I probably do." She hooked her arm through his, and they began walking back toward her place. "But first, how has Amberly done today?"

"I made sure she didn't give Vanessa a hard time."

"That's a good start. Where is Amberly now?"

"She's playing ring-around-the-rosy with some of the kids. She's really good with them, actually."

"Good. I'm glad she had a better day." Charlie glanced at her watch as if she had something else coming up. "I have about two hours until I need to leave again."

"Where are you going this time?"

"I have a horse to rescue."

He dropped his head to the side. "Tonight?"

"It can't wait."

"Why don't you send Jesse or Hudson?"

"Because this is what I do, not them."

"But with everything you have going on . . ."

Charlie squeezed his arm. "It'll be fine. I just need to grab a bite to eat, and we can talk."

Monroe wished he could convince her to change her mind.

But he knew he couldn't.

Instead, they walked into Charlie's place, and he prepared himself for whatever update she had to tell him.

———

Over a dinner of roast beef and mashed potatoes at Charlie's place, she finished filling Monroe in on what happened. He listened attentively to each detail.

Then he shared what had happened with him today—including his conversation with Jesse about Detective Vincent. He also mentioned that he'd talked with Jonathan.

"Thank you." Charlie pushed her half-eaten plate of food away. "I really appreciate that. I'm tempted to let the boy go."

"I don't think he has bad intentions. I think he's just letting his hormones talk."

Charlie scowled. "That's even more reason to let him go."

"Maybe just let it play out a little longer first?" Monroe gently suggested.

Charlie nodded and glanced at the time again

before standing. "I've got to head out if I'm going to get there before it's too late."

"Why don't you let me go with you?" Monroe asked.

"It'll be too much for you."

"I'm not that fragile," he told her.

"I need you to be healthy. Okay?" Charlie tried to express to him with her gaze just how important this was to her.

Finally, he nodded. "But you're going by yourself? I don't know if that's a good idea."

"I think it's better if I go alone. I'll slip in and out, and I'll be careful. I've done this a hundred times before. I know how to be sneaky."

"Where are you going?" a new voice demanded.

Charlie looked over her shoulder. She hadn't even heard the front door open.

But Amberly stood there.

How much of the conversation had she overheard?

"I have a horse rescue to do tonight," Charlie explained.

Amberly stepped closer. "Take me with you."

Charlie thought about it only a split second before shaking her head. "That's not a good idea."

"I can do it. I love horses. I want to help."

She stared at Amberly another moment, unsure how to respond.

Sometimes Charlie got herself into some sticky situations doing these rescues. She didn't want to put Amberly in that position also.

"It's a bad idea," Charlie finally said.

Hope faded from Amberly's eyes, and her shoulders slumped as a pout stretched across her face. "You're never going to let me do anything to help you, are you?"

"I heard you were playing with some of the kids today. That's a huge help."

"But I want to do big, important things."

"Big, important things start with small, seemingly inconsequential things."

Amberly gave her a pointed look. "You do hate me, don't you?"

"Of course, I don't hate you. I want to keep you safe." Charlie's voice began to rise.

"If this is dangerous, then why are you going alone?"

"Because I'm a big girl," Charlie said.

Amberly let out an aggravated grunt.

Charlie exchanged a glance with Monroe. Something lingered in his gaze . . . some thought he was keeping quiet.

Did he think Amberly should go with her?

She remembered what he'd said last night. Something about how Charlie and Amberly needed to find middle ground, something that would bond them.

Could that be a horse rescue? She'd gotten herself into some scrapes before, but she'd never really been in danger.

Besides, for this horse—Sammy was her name—she'd sent Mateo over earlier to check things out.

He'd offered to buy the horse, but the owner—an older, frail man—had refused and told him to get off his property.

The owner had been nasty, but he'd also had some stubborn pride, Mateo said.

The truth was that the man probably needed help himself.

But the horse needed more help and didn't have the option of asking for it. That's why Charlie wanted to step in.

Sometimes in the process of saving others—humans or animals—you learned a little more about saving yourself.

That's how it had worked for Charlie, at least.

Charlie still had her doubts but finally she sighed. "Okay, you can come."

Amberly's eyes lit. "Really?"

"Really. But I need you to change into something less obvious than what you're wearing now." She nodded at the bright pink shirt Amberly wore. "You have to promise to listen to me and not try to do things your way."

"I promise I'll listen."

Charlie nodded. "Then we need to hit the road."

Amberly squealed before rushing toward her room.

Charlie bit down as she watched the girl disappear.

She prayed she didn't regret this.

AFTER CHARLIE HOOKED the horse trailer to her Humvee, she and Amberly started down a dark desert road. For the next thirty miles, the two of them would be surrounded by miles and miles of nothing.

Charlie found a small amount of comfort in the openness, but she knew not everyone did.

Out here, people could see them coming from miles away.

They'd have to be careful as they approached the ranch.

Charlie would need to cut her headlights. But she'd also need to get close—close enough that they could put the horse in the trailer.

This wasn't her preferred way of doing things— sneaking around at night and absconding with the horses.

This was always a last resort.

Charlie hoped Amberly understood that.

It was hard to tell.

Awkwardness stretched between them.

What should Charlie even say? She wasn't usually at a loss for words, but this situation had her rattled.

Amberly beat her to it. "So . . . you like Monroe?"

The question startled Charlie, and she did a double take. "What?"

"Monroe . . . are the two of you going to get married?"

"What? No. We're . . . ." What were they? "We're just friends."

"Oh, come on." Amberly rolled her eyes. "Anyone can see that you're more than friends. And he is hot with a capital H-A-W-T."

Charlie held back a chuckle at Amberly's verbiage. "There's more to a person than being hot."

"So you're saying he's hot but has poor character?"

"No, of course not!" Monroe was one of the best men Charlie knew.

"Then what's there not to like?"

Charlie wasn't used to being the one interrogated.

And she didn't like it.

Her back muscles tightened so quickly they might snap.

"It's complicated," Charlie finally said.

"That's what adults always say when they don't want to talk about something." Amberly gave her a pointed look.

"Well, I'm glad to know he has your stamp of approval."

"Sometimes I think he's the only one at the ranch who gets me."

"Is that right?" Charlie didn't know what to think about that. But she was glad Amberly felt as if she could trust Monroe—because she could.

"He even tossed around a football with me today. It was the most normal moment I've had since I got here."

Charlie smiled at the thought of the two of them bonding.

If only Charlie could find that magic thing that would bring her and Amberly closer. "Did you know he used to play professionally?"

"No, he didn't tell me that. But he looks like the type who could've been a professional, as big as he is. How did the two of you guys meet anyway?"

Again, this wasn't something Charlie talked about very often.

She released a long breath as she collected her

thoughts. "So . . . actually, Monroe knew your grandfather from when they played football."

"Isn't Monroe a lot younger?"

"Yes, my father was considered old for the game, but he was so successful that he was never cut, even though he was in his mid-thirties. Monroe was a rookie."

"Is Monroe older than you then?"

"Six years older. I was sixteen when my father died. Monroe was twenty-two and married."

Amberly's eyes widened. "He's been married before?"

"He has. It didn't end very well."

"Did it end when he met you?"

"What?" Charlie's voice came out high-pitched. "No, I never met him when he was married. In fact, I didn't meet him until three years ago."

Amberly settled back in her seat. "So, how'd you meet then?"

Charlie swallowed hard again as they bounced down the road. "At the time, I'd already purchased the old dude ranch and had hired a couple of cowboys to help me."

"You mean the beefy, former law enforcement ones?"

Charlie smiled at Amberly's description. "No, I mean just regular ranch hands who could help me with the horses. But I knew I wanted to do more with the place."

"And?"

"Anyway . . . I was doing some regular speaking circuits to talk about my father's legacy."

"You mean like public speaking?" Amberly made a face. "I always hated having to do that at school."

"You get used to it. I did it all over the States, and I did quite well at it. *And* I made a lot of great contacts."

Amberly nodded knowingly. "Now it makes sense. You're one of those people who are good at networking."

"I actually hate networking, but it's a necessary evil. While I was doing a speaking engagement in Dallas, Monroe heard I was in town. He asked to meet with me for dinner to talk about my dad. I said yes."

"Was it a date?" Her eyebrows flung up almost comically.

"No, not a date. Nothing of the sort."

"So why did he want to meet?"

"He wanted to tell me how much my father meant to him. How he'd helped change his life."

"That was . . . nice." Amberly shrugged at the unexpected twist.

"He had his own business—a private security

firm. He also had a master's degree in business. And he was a stand-up guy. During our talk, I realized he was the person I'd been looking for."

"As a life partner?"

"No! Not as a life partner. But I knew in order to make Vanishing Ranch work, I'd need to surround myself with the right people."

"And Monroe was the right person." She nodded.

"I needed someone to be my right-hand man. To offer security. To be a sounding board. To give me business advice. He fit every box that I needed checked."

"You asked him to come aboard just like that? Did he hesitate?"

"He told me to give him a few days. He called back the next day and said yes."

"Wow. That's kind of cool. You must've intrigued him. He's been here ever since?"

"That's right."

Charlie glanced at her rearview mirror and saw headlights behind her.

Her back muscles tightened.

The vehicle had come out of nowhere. When she and Amberly had left the ranch, they hadn't been followed. Charlie had made sure of it.

This could be another rancher heading back from a trip into town.

But she needed to be careful.

"What's wrong? Why do you look so concerned?" Amberly glanced behind her. "Wait . . . are those people following us?"

"No . . . of course not." Her throat tightened when she realized she might not be telling the truth.

"You don't sound convinced of that."

Why could this girl read her so easily? It was unnerving, to be honest.

Charlie glanced in the mirror again.

The headlights disappeared . . . because the driver was entirely too close to the horse trailer.

She stomped on the gas.

A harsh nudge jolted them.

The Humvee and trailer began to jackknife.

Then Charlie and Amberly began to careen off the road.

———

Charlie heard the crunch of metal. Felt the vehicle veering out of control.

It didn't matter how she pressed the brakes or turned the wheel.

Nothing she did seemed to help.

Then she felt the rumble of the road beneath her.

No, not the road.

They were off the road and bumping across the desert.

Don't tip, she prayed. *Please don't tip.*

Amberly screamed beside her, and Charlie gripped the wheel harder.

Then a huge rock formation appeared in front of them.

She hit the brakes harder, even though she knew it would do no good.

The next moment, the Hummer slammed into the rock.

The impact jolted Charlie forward.

Her forehead hit the steering wheel.

And everything went black.

"CHARLIE. Charlie. You've got to wake up!"

Charlie felt someone shaking her. Heard a familiar voice. Heard the panic.

She groaned and tried to open her eyes.

But her head hurt so bad.

"Charlie . . . wake up!" someone said.

Amberly, she realized.

Amberly was with her.

At once, everything rushed back to her.

That driver had run them off the road. They'd jackknifed. Hit the rock.

Charlie's heart sped, and her eyes flung open.

She glanced at the darkness around her, and Amberly's face came into view. "Are you okay?"

"I don't know. I don't know." Tears flooded the girl's gaze.

"Are you hurt?"

Amberly quickly scanned herself. "I . . . I don't think so."

"How long was I out?"

"Only a few seconds."

Alarm raced through Charlie. "That means the other driver could still be here. I can't let him get to us right now. Stay here and stay down. Do you understand?"

Charlie reached for the gun beneath her jacket.

"Wait . . . you're not leaving me here, are you?" Amberly rushed.

She paused. "I'm not going far."

"But . . ." Amberly grabbed her arm, panic in her gaze.

"Call the guys at Vanishing Ranch. I programmed their numbers into your phone. Tell them what happened. Okay?"

Amberly stared at her another moment before nodding. "Okay. But . . . I'm . . . I'm scared."

Charlie squeezed her arm. "I know. Me too."

With one last look at her, Charlie opened the door.

She stepped onto the dry ground and pressed her eyes closed as her head began to swirl. After sucking in several deep breaths, she finally righted herself and glanced around.

She couldn't see the road because of the way the trailer had landed.

But she could barely make out headlight beams creeping around the back of the trailer.

The other driver was still here, wasn't he? Waiting to see if Charlie and Amberly had survived. Maybe waiting to finish them both off.

Charlie gripped her gun tighter.

She should have asked someone else to come with her. It hadn't been a smart move to come without backup. Now it could get Amberly killed.

She chided herself for the decision.

Remaining near the edge of the vehicle, Charlie crept toward the trailer.

Her hands trembled with anticipation.

She was equipped to do many things.

But if she was outnumbered right now . . . then she and Amberly were both sitting ducks.

Finally, she reached the horse trailer. She snuck along the side of it, only raising her head to try to get a glimpse through the windows.

But the headlights on the other side were so glaring that she couldn't see anything else.

Charlie ducked again and edged toward the end of the trailer.

This was it.

The moment she would step out.

Just as she cleared the trailer and spotted the SUV that hit her, she heard an engine rev.

Then the vehicle barreled toward her.

———

Charlie threw herself to the side as the car raced in her direction.

She hit the ground, but she was still exposed as the driver rushed her way.

Headlights blinded her.

Any moment now, she'd be crushed.

She braced herself for the impact.

But, at the last moment, the vehicle swerved.

It zoomed away, leaving a trail of dust.

Charlie released her breath, her heart still racing.

That had been a warning, hadn't it?

Whoever that driver was, he could have killed her.

But he'd chosen not to.

The message was loud and clear. If Charlie kept looking into this, next time she wouldn't be as lucky.

As she pulled herself to her feet, Amberly appeared beside her. "Are you okay?"

"I told you to stay in the car," Charlie said with a moan.

"I couldn't stay in there if you were out here dying!"

Charlie counted to three before responding. "I need to know I can trust you when I tell you to do something."

"I just wanted to help!"

Charlie's head pounded. She knew the girl was coming from a good place. She also knew that Amberly needed to learn to listen if she was going to participate in any of these horse rescues with her.

"Give me a hand up." Charlie extended her arm.

Amberly stared at her hand a moment before finally reaching out to help her to her feet.

Charlie shoved her gun back into its holster and watched as the taillights disappeared in the distance. Then she wiped the dust from her jeans and glanced at the trailer.

"Looks like the axle is bent on this." She knelt for a better look but felt a rush of lightheadedness.

She drew in a deep breath to keep her head from spinning.

"That's not good, is it?" Amberly frowned. "How are we going to rescue Sammy?"

"We're not going to be able to. Not tonight."

"But . . ." Disappointment saturated Amberly's gaze.

"We're lucky to be alive right now. And it's not as if we can put the horse in the back of the Hummer."

Amberly pouted a moment before crossing her arms. Then she glanced up at Charlie and cringed. "You're bleeding from your forehead."

Charlie reached for the cut and felt the blood there.

"It's just a head wound."

"Just a head wound?" Amberly stared at her as if she'd lost her mind.

"It's a line from a movie. *Monty Python?*"

Amberly stared at Charlie as if she'd grown a third eye.

Charlie waved the reference off. This wasn't the time to explain.

She had other things to worry about.

TWENTY-SIX

"I'VE GOT to figure out how we're going to get out of here," Charlie muttered as she glanced around.

Her headlights illuminated the large rock in front of her, but she could see little beyond that.

"For real." Amberly shivered. "I watched this movie one time where these people got stuck in the desert, and all these mutants who'd been deformed by a radioactive event in the desert emerged from the hills and did all these horrible things to them."

"There are no radioactive mutants out here. I can promise you that." A brief image of some men who'd dressed as lizard people to search for fallen meteorites filled Charlie's mind. Thankfully, they'd just been wearing costumes.

No, there were people who were much more real

and much more dangerous. But Charlie didn't share that with Amberly.

"Did you talk to anyone at Vanishing Ranch?" Charlie asked.

"There's no cell signal out here."

Charlie frowned. Of course. She should have known.

She paced toward the front of the Hummer. "Let me see if I can get this started."

She'd almost taken an SUV instead of the Humvee, but she was so glad she hadn't.

Any other car would've crumpled after hitting that rock.

But the Humvee appeared to have only a few dents.

Charlie climbed into the driver's seat and tried to start the engine.

It sputtered, but nothing happened.

She released the hood and climbed back out to look at the engine.

She found the switch near the fuel pump that had flipped after the accident and maneuvered it back in place.

"How did you learn to do stuff like this?" Amberly stood close, watching everything.

"I was on my own for a long time. It was either I

got things done or things didn't get done. That period of my life taught me to be independent."

"That's one way to look at it."

"I've learned that you can either take what life gives you and cry about it. Or you can take what life gives you and make it work in your favor."

She jiggled a few more wires and then told Amberly to climb into the driver's seat.

"Really?" The teen looked at her.

"Really. You know how to start a car?"

"I may have done it a few times."

Charlie wondered what the story was behind that. "Remember to put your foot on the brake first. Then see if it will turn over."

Amberly climbed in the vehicle and pushed the ignition button.

As the engine roared to life, Amberly let out a squeal. "It worked!"

"Perfect. Don't turn it off. I'm going to disconnect this trailer, and then we need to head back to the ranch."

"You're just going to leave the trailer here?"

"We have to. I'll send a crew out tomorrow to get it for me. Right now we need to get back." *It's not safe out here.* But Charlie didn't add that last part.

She didn't think those guys would return tonight.

Then again, Charlie hadn't thought they would follow her out here either.

———

Monroe had been pacing all evening as he waited for Charlie to get back.

He should have insisted on going with her. Or insisted on sending someone else.

But it was too late for that.

Even worse was the fact that out in the middle of the desert there was no cell phone reception. So if something happened to her . . .

He glanced at his watch. Charlie and Amberly had only been gone an hour.

That wasn't long enough to grow worried.

But he was.

Monroe gave up his pacing in favor of sitting in a rocking chair on the porch in front of the mess hall. No sooner had he sat down did headlights flash in the distance.

Was Charlie back already? No one else was due to come tonight.

The gates opened, and the Hummer pulled inside.

Charlie's Hummer.

He rose and went to meet her.

But as the vehicle came to a stop near the house, he noticed the horse trailer was no longer behind it.

His heart raced faster.

Then he saw the dent on the front bumper.

His muscles tensed.

A moment later, Charlie and Amberly stepped out.

A trace amount of blood dripped down Charlie's forehead.

Something had happened out there.

His gaze shifted to Amberly, but the girl appeared unharmed.

He placed his hands on his hips as he waited, his self-control the only thing stopping him from demanding answers.

Charlie paused in front of him and frowned. "Things didn't go as planned."

"I can see that. Are you okay?"

"As well as I can be."

He turned to Amberly. "And you?"

She nodded, something that almost looked like excitement or adrenaline glimmering in her gaze. "Charlie was pretty amazing out there when those guys ran us off the road."

His heart quickened. "What?"

"I'll explain in a minute." Charlie turned to Amberly. "Why don't you go inside and get a shower so you can turn in for the night? It's been a very long day."

Amberly nodded and started for the house. Before stepping inside, she turned back to Charlie, and her expression sobered. "I'm glad you're okay."

A small smile feathered across Charlie's face. "I'm glad you're okay also."

Monroe noted the moment. Maybe whatever had happened bonded the two.

But that wasn't what he meant when he'd said they needed to find common ground.

As Amberly slipped inside, Monroe turned to Charlie. "What happened out there?"

She frowned before pulling her lips into a tight line. "Why don't we go inside to talk? I'd like to sit down."

That sounded like a good idea.

TWENTY-SEVEN

CHARLIE SHIFTED beside Monroe as they sat on the couch.

His intense gaze zeroed in on her.

A surprising rush of nerves swept through her.

Why was that? She'd never cared what people thought of her. It was one of her survival mechanisms, she supposed.

But for some reason she *did* care about what Monroe thought.

She'd known that for a while; she'd simply never acknowledged it.

She was keenly aware of his every movement, his every touch.

"So, what happened?" Monroe squirted antiseptic cream on some gauze and began to pat her wound.

As he did, she ran through the story, not leaving out any details.

"Charlie . . . you could've been killed." He paused and stared at her.

She shrugged. "I know. I could have been. But that driver didn't want me dead. He or she just wanted to give me a warning."

He sighed before placing a butterfly bandage on her cut. Then set the first aid kit on the table and turned toward her, giving Charlie his full attention.

"I don't like how any of this is going," he said. "The more you keep pushing, the more these people will want to eliminate you."

"I know, but I can't back off now. I'm too close. And isn't that the problem? These guys scare off anyone who gets too close, so the truth doesn't come out. So they're not exposed."

"You have contacts in law enforcement agencies all across the country. You could let them handle this."

"I don't know who's in the pocket of these people. I don't trust anyone."

"No one?"

Charlie shrugged as she looked at him. "I mean, I trust everyone here. I trust you."

Their gazes locked.

"I'm glad to hear that," Monroe murmured. "Because I can't stand the thought of losing you."

The concern in his eyes caused something to crack inside her.

She tried not to think about losing people she cared about. But she'd come so close to losing Monroe.

When that had happened, Charlie had realized the reality of their jobs and what they did. The reality that the people she cared about could be taken from her at any minute.

Yet part of her still tried to keep Monroe at a distance.

Why? She was already in too deep. She already cared about him.

She was simply living in denial now.

She cleared her throat as some inward urge pushed her to speak. "Monroe . . . when you were in the hospital . . ."

She couldn't finish her statement. Instead, tears rolled down her cheeks.

"I'm not in the hospital anymore," Monroe muttered.

"I know. But when you were . . . I thought . . . I was afraid . . ."

"Shh." He leaned closer. "You don't have to finish if you don't want to."

"I thought I was going to lose you too," she finally said.

Monroe's arms enveloped her as he pulled her to his chest. "Everything is okay now."

Charlie let herself melt into him. He stroked her back and murmured words of comfort.

The man was so tough yet so tender also. The combination mesmerized her.

Monroe didn't even realize how much he meant to her.

Why was that?

She knew. It was because she'd never told him.

Charlie needed to change that.

She straightened so she could look him in the eyes. But her breath caught before she could say anything.

The emotion in his gaze caused her heart to leap into her throat.

It was one of the few times in her life she actually felt speechless.

"You take care of everyone else, Charlie," he murmured. "But who's going to take care of you?"

"I can take care of myself." Her words came out scratchy.

"It comes to a point where we can't be that solitary."

She shrugged as she tried to keep her emotions intact. "Maybe."

Monroe's arms tightened around her waist. "I'd like to volunteer for that job."

Charlie's heartbeat quickened as his words settled on her. "Would you?"

"I've been jockeying for the position for a while."

Something in her heart felt like it had cracked. Like tension had been building inside it for years and years.

Now with one conversation, her defenses were crumbling, and her walls were coming down.

As she stared into Monroe's eyes, she finally threw caution to the wind.

She leaned toward him and pressed her lips against his.

Monroe didn't hesitate. He pulled her closer, and his lips claimed hers. The tension growing between them for all these months seemed to be released in the kiss.

The kiss that continued.

And continued.

Until finally the door behind them opened, and someone said, "Eww . . . get a room."

Amberly.

Charlie and Monroe eased away from each other and exchanged a glance.

Then they burst into laughter. Charlie was supposed to be the one catching Amberly kissing, not vice versa.

Charlie couldn't remember the last time she'd felt like such a teenager.

For once, it was a good feeling.

———

Monroe and Charlie waited until Amberly grabbed some water from the kitchen.

The girl seemed to keep one eye on them with everything she did.

Charlie had moved away from Monroe—though only slightly—with one arm draped behind the couch as she still leaned close.

Monroe's heart pounded out of control.

He'd dreamed for so long about what it would be like to kiss Charlie.

And it was even better than he'd ever imagined.

It only made him want more.

He wanted to let her know how much he loved her. Always and forever.

He wanted everyone to know.

He'd never felt so strongly about something.

Never.

Finally, Amberly gave them one last glance and then held up her glass of water. "Carry on!"

Then she went into her room and closed the door.

As soon as she disappeared, Charlie let out a laugh and leaned into him, nestling her head in the crook of his neck and shoulder. She wrapped her arms around his waist, and Monroe couldn't help but note how snuggly the two of them fit together.

"What are we doing, Monroe?" she asked softly.

"I know what I want this to be." There was no need to skirt around the truth. He'd done that for too long now.

"What's that?" She nudged her head up just enough to look him in the eyes.

"I've loved you from the moment I met you, Charlie Soldier." His voice sounded hoarse with emotion, but he didn't try to hide it. Not anymore.

Her eyes widened as warmth flooded her gaze. "You have?"

"You couldn't tell?" He'd thought it was so obvious.

Her bright smile faded as another thought seemed to enter her mind. "I largely try to avoid relationships."

"I know."

"You do too," Charlie said.

He shrugged, unable to deny it. "My first marriage was a disaster."

"All my past relationships have been."

"But I think you and I could be different."

Her soft grin returned. "Me too."

As their gazes locked, they leaned toward each other.

Their lips met in another kiss.

One that Monroe never wanted to end.

TWENTY-EIGHT

THE NEXT MORNING, Charlie called a meeting in the conference room with Monroe, Suzy, Jesse, and Hudson.

She'd woken up with a new spring in her step, and she practically felt herself blush every time she glanced at Monroe.

Their kisses last night had been amazing. But even more amazing was the fact that Monroe cared about her just as much as she cared about him. Charlie nearly felt like pinching herself.

But she couldn't dwell on those things now.

There were other matters she had to attend to.

Standing at the front of the conference table, Charlie observed Suzy a moment as the woman sat across the table. Charlie noted the hollow circles beneath her eyes.

As per their procedure here at Vanishing Ranch, the woman's belongings had been checked when she arrived.

There had been no drugs found on her. But Charlie was still fairly certain Suzy was withdrawing from some kind of substance.

Thankfully, Charlie had counselors on hand that could help the woman with that process.

Charlie glanced at her watch. She was waiting for one more person to show up before they started this meeting. He should be here at any time.

When she heard the *whomp whomp* of a helicopter in the distance, she knew her guest had arrived.

Several moments later, Bentley Prescott stepped into the room.

The man was on the shorter side, but he carried himself like someone twice his size. He had faded blond hair that receded from his forehead, even though he was only in his mid-thirties. His eyes were brown and intelligent, and his actions confident and assured.

He nodded at Charlie before taking a seat near the head of the table.

"Everyone," Charlie started. "This is Bentley Prescott. He's an attorney with the FBI."

Looks of surprise and admiration went around the table.

"He's agreed to come here today—with Suzy's permission—so he can help us form our next plan of action," Charlie continued.

"Charlie's friends, Wallace and Greta, were like parents to me growing up." Bentley turned to the group around him. "When I heard Charlie needed something, I knew I needed to give it a listen."

Charlie swallowed hard. She'd been mentally reviewing how this meeting would go ever since she set it up last night.

Now she hoped it didn't get derailed.

"Suzy, as we talked about earlier, I'm hoping that you wouldn't mind sharing what you told me with Bentley and the rest of the group." Charlie glanced at the woman and nodded reassuringly.

Suzy's eyes skittered about nervously, but she bobbed her head up and down.

Then she launched into the same story she'd told Charlie yesterday.

Everyone at the table listened with rapt attention to what she said.

Bentley took notes but didn't show any other emotion or give any hint as to what he thought about all this.

Finally, Suzy ended her story with her flight here to the ranch yesterday.

Bentley jotted down a few more things before

lowering his pen and looking up at Suzy. "You're a very brave woman for sharing all that. Thank you."

"What do you think?" Charlie nearly held her breath as she waited for his response.

"I think you've got the start of a decent case." He nodded slowly, his expression still pensive.

Relief swept through her.

But Bentley quickly added, "I'm just not sure we have enough yet." He turned back to Suzy. "You said you'd be willing to go on record? To testify if this went to trial?"

She nodded.

"That's a great start," Bentley continued. "But unfortunately, it's going to be your word against anyone that we may put on trial. The defense would decimate your character."

Suzy's gaze fell.

"She'd been forced into that lifestyle." Protectiveness rose in Charlie. "How could anyone hold that against her?"

But even as she asked the question, she knew the truth of the matter. She knew how the system worked. Those who needed the most help were usually dismissed. The victims often remained unseen while all the focus went on the person doing the crime.

"So what else do we need to bring this case

against these people?" Monroe shifted, his intense gaze on Bentley.

"We have copies of the pictures and the interviews that Charlie sent me. Those are definitely a good start. But we need something concrete and not circumstantial. None of these things point back directly to the bombing."

"But there's enough there to raise doubt, reasonable doubt," Charlie said.

He stared at the pictures of President Radar again. "You may be right. But we're going to need more."

———

As everyone took a break for lunch an hour later, Suzy lingered back in the conference room. Charlie stayed with her.

She sat beside the woman, anxious to get a pulse on how she was feeling. Today had to be exhausting for her—and disappointing.

"You did great," Charlie started.

Suzy kept her gaze averted as she nodded. "Thank you."

"I know that wasn't easy."

"It wasn't. But I know I need to do something. I've been quiet about this for too long. Living in fear for as long as I can remember."

Another question had lingered in Charlie's mind, something she'd nearly forgotten about with everything else that had happened.

But it seemed worth bringing up.

"Suzy, does the name Lothario mean anything to you?"

When Suzy looked up, her face looked even paler than before, and a tremble shook her body. "I . . . well, yes. That's the name of the ringleader."

Charlie's breath caught. "It is?"

Then why hadn't Suzy mentioned that sooner? It seemed like an important detail to add.

Suzy seemed to read her thoughts and rushed, "That's not his real name. That's just what people called him. I didn't think it had much significance."

"You said that you have no idea who he is?"

"That's right. Like I said, it's someone high-level and untouchable."

"In other words, it's someone with money and power." Charlie frowned as she said the words.

She'd known that from the start, however. But she kept getting more and more confirmations of it.

Who was this guy?

And how were they going to find enough evidence to put him and everyone affiliated with his dirty little business behind bars?

MONROE KNEW he had to be careful not to overdo it. He was feeling exhausted, but he could still get through these meetings. It was important that he was there, that he helped.

He spotted Charlie talking to Bentley in the corner and stepped up to join them, hoping he wasn't imposing.

When he saw the bright smile light up Charlie's face, he knew he wasn't.

Seeing that smile gave him a new reason to get up every day.

She rested her hand in the crook of his arm and gave it a squeeze. "Are you feeling okay?"

He nodded. "Just fine."

Bentley shifted toward him. "Look, I wasn't sure

if I should bring this up or not. But tonight I need to be back in DC for a soirée I'm attending."

"Okay." Charlie waited for him to continue, a touch of confusion in her voice.

"Bill Radar is supposed to be there. I'm not saying it's a good idea if you come or not. I *am* saying that it could be an opportunity for you to talk to him."

"It's not too late to get tickets?" Charlie's voice lilted with hope.

"I could get you in as a guest."

Monroe didn't like the thought of that. Would Charlie be this guy's date? Where exactly did Monroe and Charlie stand?

They hadn't talked about it. Was their kiss just a kiss?

He swallowed the thoughts. He and Charlie could talk about that later.

Charlie nodded at Monroe. "And Monroe?"

Bentley glanced up at him, and a barely perceptible frown tugged at his lips. "I can probably get him in too."

"Are you feeling up to it?" Charlie's gaze connected with his.

"You know it."

He saw the lingering questions in her gaze—questions about whether he could handle it.

He could. In fact, nothing would stop him.

"What time does it start?" Charlie pushed ahead as if she didn't notice Bentley's disappointment that Charlie wouldn't be on his arm.

"Eight."

She glanced at her watch. "That means we don't have a lot of time to get ready and catch the plane."

"So you're in?" Bentley stared at her.

She nodded. "I am most definitely in."

"Very well. I'll make arrangements." Bentley pulled out his phone and stepped away.

When the man was occupied, Monroe stepped closer to Charlie.

She was making this seem so simple. But he had concerns about this whole thing.

"Are you sure this is a good idea?" he whispered. "You don't know what you're getting yourself into."

"But you'll be there with me."

"I will. But . . ." He wanted to be his normal self. But he knew he wasn't there yet.

He'd protect Charlie with everything he had but . . . what if that wasn't enough?

She rested her hand on his chest, almost as if she sensed his rising anxiety and racing heartbeat. "I'll be fine."

He swallowed hard as he felt her so close. It made him want to pull her even closer. To kiss her again.

To somehow forget about all the problems at hand.

If only he could . . .

Instead, he asked, "What exactly do you hope to accomplish?"

She let out a long exhale before shaking her head. "I'm not sure. I'll figure that out later. Right now, I need to find a dress, and you need to get your tux ready."

Monroe nodded, but he already dreaded what the rest of the day would hold.

Charlie felt the flutter of nerves sweep through her as she and Monroe pulled up to the massive house where the soirée was being held.

The place was at least ten thousand square feet and appeared immaculate with its manicured lawn and stately entry.

She knew it was risky coming here.

She knew someone wanted to silence her.

It could very well be somebody at the party right now.

Bentley had told her about several people on the guest list.

There were definitely people here tonight who Suzy had named.

Charlie and Monroe could be walking into the lion's den.

But how could she pass up this opportunity?

She couldn't.

They climbed from the limo she'd hired to drive them here from the airport and paused. She turned to Monroe and gazed at him a moment in his tux. Looking at him now, no one would ever know he'd been on the verge of losing his life a couple of weeks prior.

"You look amazing," she murmured.

She wanted to lean in closer. Get another whiff of his spicy cologne. Find another burst of strength in his touch.

But this wasn't the time or place.

Monroe took her hand and swirled her around. "You are the one who looks amazing."

She'd wanted to wear her favorite red dress, but she feared she'd stand out too much if she did. Instead, she'd picked a simple black gown that hugged her curves and stretched down to her ankles with a modest split on the side.

She paused just long enough to straighten the collar of Monroe's tux—not that it needed to be straightened. It was just a nervous gesture, she supposed.

She reached up and kissed him on the cheek before looping her arm through his. "Now we need to get inside."

"Yes, ma'am."

They stepped into the sweeping mansion owned by long-standing senator Erwin Rodgers. The man came from old family money and was an expert in the political game.

Inside, they paused and glanced at all the people mingling.

If things had turned out differently in Charlie's life, this could be her normal social scene.

She was so glad that it wasn't.

She much preferred ranch life.

She recognized several faces already. Not because they were people she knew necessarily. But they were people that she knew of.

And she knew many attendees would recognize her as well from when she'd spoken at fundraisers about her father's legacy. She'd made several magazine covers and had been interviewed on national news programs. Her face was recognizable.

"Where do we start?" Monroe murmured as they stood on the edge of the crowd.

"That's a good question." Charlie needed to

figure out the best people they could begin to mingle with.

Before she could decide, Bentley approached them. "So . . . you did make it."

"Here we are." Charlie held up a hand. "I think we clean up pretty nicely."

He looked her up and down. "Yes, you do. But you need to be careful here tonight. On the outside, these people are full of decorum. But what lies beneath that . . . is anyone's guess."

Charlie repressed a shiver. She didn't like the sound of that.

But now it was time to get busy.

"IF IT ISN'T CHARLIE SOLDIER." Former President Radar stopped beside them. His gaze then went to Monroe. "And you played for the Patriots for a few seasons, correct? Back before their Super Bowl days."

"That's right." Monroe tried to keep his muscles loose.

"It's good to see you again, President Radar." Charlie nodded at him. "It's been a while."

"It most definitely has been. I thought you were out of this scene."

She shrugged. "I am . . . mostly. Occasionally, I like to remind people that I'm still around."

"I'm sure that's something people aren't likely to forget." He flashed what Monroe called his "campaign smile," his focus on Charlie. "What have you been up to lately? I hope you're still speaking. You always did such a wonderful job."

Charlie shrugged again, looking at ease even in the midst of the high-stakes situation. "Funny you should ask. I've actually been devoting a lot of my time into researching the Overland Hotel bombing."

Monroe tried not to show his surprise.

He hadn't expected Charlie to be so direct.

Then again, the woman was full of surprises.

Monroe observed Radar's expression. Took note of how the man looked a little paler now.

"Is that right?" Radar shifted. "Why would you do that? The FBI closed the case on that a long time ago."

"I think they were wrong." Charlie said the words with 100 percent confidence.

"Well, I suppose there's nothing wrong with a good conspiracy theory." He let out a nervous chuckle.

"If that's what you want to call it." Charlie didn't bother to hide the challenge in her gaze.

Radar swallowed hard, some of his polished façade fading. "What exactly is your conspiracy?"

"My theory is that powerful men made the bombing look like an act of terrorism in order to conceal their own lewd acts."

His face went still before he let out another stran-gled chuckle. "That's quite a theory."

"Since we're talking—" Before Charlie could finish her statement, Radar's wife appeared and hooked her arms through his.

"I'm sorry to interrupt, but I really need Bill over here a moment to settle a debate for us," the woman said with a stiff smile.

"Of course." Charlie returned the stiff smile.

As Bill and his wife walked away, Bill called over his shoulder, "Good luck with your theory."

Monroe waited until Radar was out of earshot until he said, "That was bold."

Charlie stepped closer, her gaze still on the former president. "This isn't a time to be timid. He already knows that I know. He was just surprised I spoke about it so freely."

"How do you know?" Monroe asked as they began walking between the guests lingering in the large foyer.

"Just a gut feeling."

"We need more than gut feelings to file charges against these men."

A frown tugged at her lips. "I know. I'm still working on that. That's why we came here tonight." She paused and glanced around. "But none of these people are going to talk to us and admit anything."

"So why are we here?"

"To show that I'm not going to back down or be intimidated."

He had to give the woman credit—she was a real pistol. But that would also make her a target. He didn't like that thought.

Charlie paused and opened the small clutch she carried. "I don't know where Bentley went. I wonder if he found out anything. Maybe he sent me a message."

But as she peered inside the narrow opening for her phone, she flinched.

Monroe leaned closer. "What is it?"

"There's an envelope in here." She glanced around. "I don't know where it came from. I haven't set down my purse since we walked in."

Monroe's back muscles tensed as he scanned everyone around them. How had someone managed to slip something into Charlie's purse without them noticing?

He didn't like the thought of that. He and Charlie were both alert and aware—much more so than the average person.

Charlie nodded toward the hallway. "Let's go somewhere private to open this."

———

Charlie felt a tremble of nerves as they stepped into a bedroom off the living area.

At least, if she and Monroe were caught, they could come up with some type of flimsy excuse as to what they were doing in here. Hopefully, people wouldn't ask them any questions or notice they were missing.

"I'll stand guard near the door," Monroe said. "Just in case."

Charlie walked to the dresser where she flipped on a small lamp.

But her hands trembled as she held the envelope. She hoped that Monroe couldn't see how nervous she felt.

Carefully, she opened the seal. She wanted to be careful how much of it she touched just in case there was other evidence present.

She set the envelope on the dresser and pulled out a folded sheet of beige paper.

The words inside made her reel.

Back off or I'll let the world know who your daughter's father really is.

The blood drained from her face.

Only a handful of people knew who Amberly's dad was.

One of them must be at this party.

"Everything okay?" Monroe asked from across the room.

Charlie pushed the paper away, her mind still reeling. As she did, she noticed the white powder on her fingertips.

White powder?

The next instant, her lungs seized.

She couldn't breathe.

The room spun around her.

Then she dropped to the floor.

"CHARLIE!" Monroe rushed toward her as she collapsed.

He glanced at the paper from the envelope and saw the white powder around it.

Saw the dust on her fingertips.

Instantly, he knew what it was.

Fentanyl.

He'd known for a while that people were weaponizing it.

He knew how deadly it was.

And now someone had used it on Charlie.

He patted her cheek as panic raced through him. "Charlie, wake up!"

But he knew it was no use.

Instead, he gathered her in his arms and carried her into the crowd.

He'd seen police officers in attendance earlier, offering protection to the self-proclaimed important people mingling about. He spotted one of them now standing on the fringe of the crowd and called him over.

The officer rushed toward them. "Please . . . you've got to help her. She just came in contact with fentanyl."

The officer quickly muttered something into his radio.

Meanwhile, Monroe lowered Charlie to the floor.

Several people gathered to see what the fuss was about.

As the officer bent over Charlie, the man pulled something from his pocket.

Naloxone. Monroe had heard officers were now starting to carry it.

The man popped the top off, inserted it into Charlie's nose, and squeezed. As he did, another officer pushed the crowd back and joined them.

Monroe held his breath as he watched Charlie's face, waiting for her to respond.

He knelt on the other side of her, squeezing her hand. "Come on, Charlie. You can pull through this."

But she remained unmoving.

Anger burned through him. Someone had done this on purpose.

Someone who could very well be watching—and enjoying this—right now.

"Give her another dose!" the other officer said. "We need to make sure she doesn't go into cardiac arrest!"

The first officer inserted another tube in Charlie's other nostril and then began CPR.

Sirens wailed in the distance.

Backup was on the way.

Monroe glanced around, wondering who at this party had done this to her.

"Turn her into recovery position," the first officer muttered.

Monroe closed his eyes and lifted desperate prayers.

Time seemed to stop. This was taking too long.

Charlie had to wake up. She *had* to.

I can't lose her, God. Please. Not now. Not when we've come so far. Who am I kidding? I never want to lose her . .
.

Finally, Charlie's eyes flung open, and she bent forward, gasping in a breath as life returned to her.

Monroe's shoulders sank with relief.

She was alive.

But Monroe would find the person who'd done this to her and make sure they never did anything like this again.

THIRTY-TWO

CHARLIE LAY in the hospital bed, trying to be polite to everyone who came and went.

But they were all making too big a deal over her.

She was fine.

Even so, the doctors had insisted on keeping her here for observation for a few hours.

She knew there was no way that Monroe would let her leave until the doctors gave her the okay.

He'd remained faithfully by her side every step of this ordeal. Bentley had come with them to the hospital, but he'd left a few minutes ago.

For the first time since Charlie had been brought here, it was just her and Monroe.

"Thank you." Her voice cracked as she said the words.

"Of course. I should have known . . ." Concern

etched deeply in his gaze, and his voice was hoarse with emotion.

"There was no way that either of us could have possibly known fentanyl was planted in that letter."

"But someone at the party did that to you intentionally. How did they even know you were going to be there? You were a last-minute addition."

"That's true. Only Bentley should have known."

"Unless he told someone." Monroe scowled as if he didn't like that thought.

"I don't see any way someone could have planned on leaving me that fentanyl-laced note—not when we only agreed to come at the last minute," Charlie continued. "They just happened to have a paper and envelope and that drug on them? It seems unlikely."

"Maybe we should talk to your friend Bentley one more time."

"Maybe." She squeezed Monroe's hand. "But not quite yet."

They exchanged a glance.

Charlie thought about the words written on that note.

Had Monroe read them?

Who had that note in their custody right now, for that matter? The police?

She should be the one to talk to Monroe about who Amberly's father was before anyone else did.

She licked her lips. "Monroe, there's something I should probably tell you."

"What's that?"

She licked her lips again, more nervous than she thought she would be. "It's about that letter—"

Before she could finish the sentence, a knock sounded at the door. She didn't even call, "Come in" before the person stepped inside.

Pierce.

Seeing him didn't make Charlie feel any better.

"I heard you were here." He cast a curious glance at Monroe before pausing beside her bed.

"Word must travel fast," Charlie said. "This isn't even your jurisdiction."

"When someone gets laced with fentanyl at a party thrown by a US senator, all the local PDs hear about it."

She couldn't argue with that statement. It made sense.

"Listen, can I have a moment?" Pierce cast a pointed look at Monroe.

Charlie saw Monroe bristle. He didn't like that idea.

He didn't even know about her history with Pierce, yet his instincts put him on edge.

"Just give us a few minutes." Charlie nodded at Monroe reassuringly. "I'll be fine."

But Monroe didn't budge.

"I promise I won't hurt her, big guy." Pierce almost sounded mocking as he said the words.

Something close to a low growl escaped from Monroe.

"Just wait right outside the door," Charlie said. "I'll call you if I need you."

Finally, Monroe reluctantly stepped away.

Then Charlie prepared herself for Pierce's questions.

———

Monroe didn't like being relegated to wait outside.

And he *definitely* didn't like Pierce.

Jealousy wasn't the reason either, even though he had a feeling Charlie and Pierce had been an item at one time. He even suspected that Pierce might be Amberly's dad.

But he trusted Charlie and wanted to give her the privacy she needed.

Monroe had seen the words written on that note. He'd barely comprehended them at the time because he'd been so worried about Charlie.

But someone had threatened to reveal who the father of her child was if she didn't back off.

Almost as if the reveal of Amberly's father could be scandalous.

How did Pierce fit in with that?

Monroe continued to mull over his thoughts as he leaned against the wall, biding his time while he waited for Pierce to leave.

If Charlie had given birth when she was sixteen, and if Pierce had been a couple of years older than her . . . Monroe supposed the age difference could be scandalous, and it was technically illegal.

But he sensed there was more to it than that.

Monroe wanted Charlie to give him the update. He didn't want to pry. Didn't want to make her say anything she wasn't ready to say.

But he was curious.

He shifted against the wall again and glanced down the hallway. A woman with a cleaning cart made her way from room to room. A doctor knocked on a door a few rooms down before he slipped inside. A nurse headed his way, glancing at something in her hands.

The woman quickly ducked down another hallway as soon as their gazes caught.

Monroe's muscles bristled.

It was her, he realized.

The nurse who'd visited Monroe in Phoenix and had tried to kill him.

Delilah Perkins.

She was here.

There was no telling what she was planning now.

CHAPTER
THIRTY-THREE

"WHY WOULD someone leave you that note?" Pierce asked.

Charlie stared at him, not wanting to get into this discussion. But she was trapped here in this hospital bed, and she couldn't get away. Though she hadn't wanted to tell him what the note said, she had.

"Isn't it obvious?" She resigned herself to the conversation and shrugged. "They want to scare me."

Pierce narrowed his gaze as he stared at her. "Why are they threatening you with revealing your baby daddy of all things?"

"I don't know. I guess they're desperate." Charlie kept her chin up, determined not to show any weakness.

The truth was these people knew how to hit her

vulnerabilities. It was what they did—found the painful truths about people's lives and exploited those truths for their own gain.

"Is this about your baby?"

His words hung in the air, and Charlie's throat tightened as memories filled her. "It's possible."

"Not many people knew you were pregnant."

Her jaw hardened. "I know."

"Charlie, about that—"

"I don't want to talk about my pregnancy right now." She shifted. "Do you know where that note is?"

Pierce took a step back and ran a hand over his face. "From what I heard, the police didn't find any note. They only found an envelope. They're assuming you opened the envelope and that's how you got the fentanyl in your system."

"What?" Charlie didn't know whether to be relieved or angry.

She hadn't wanted the message of that note to escape into the wild. But that meant whoever had sent it to her had gone in that bedroom behind her to retrieve it.

She repressed a shiver.

If only she'd been more lucid, maybe she could have seen who it was.

What were the odds Charlie could get her hands on any security camera footage from the party?

She knew the answer to that question.

Unlikely.

"Charlie." Pierce stepped closer. "It's clear that whatever is going on, that it's something worth killing for. We already have a string of dead reporters. The Turleys were murdered. Margaret is on death's doorstep. Someone's trying to kill you. Maybe you should back off."

She stared him in the eye. "What about you? You getting any threats?"

He frowned, and Charlie knew there was more to the story.

"The chief said I had to drop this case," he announced.

Her lips parted in surprise. "What?"

He nodded somberly. "I think someone got to him too."

"No . . ." She stared up at Pierce.

"I wish it wasn't true."

"So are you going to do it? Are you going to back off?"

He opened his mouth to respond. Before he could answer, the door opened, and Monroe darted inside.

"That nurse," he started. "She's here. The same woman who tried to kill me in Phoenix. She's in this hospital. I just tried to follow her, but I didn't want to go too far away and leave Charlie here. But you need to find her. Now."

———

After Pierce raced out the door, Monroe paced near Charlie's bed, halfway expecting trouble to barge through the door at any moment.

"Are you sure it was the same woman?" Charlie asked.

"I'm positive. These people are watching us. Following us. Just waiting for the right opportunity."

"I'm glad you were outside when you were then."

He shook his head. "I wish I could have caught her. But I wanted to stay near you."

"I appreciate the way you worry about me."

Monroe paused and strode toward her. "I don't want to see anything happen to you, Charlie."

She grabbed his hand. "Thank you for always looking out for me."

"But what if me looking out for you isn't enough?" His heart twisted as he said the words.

Monroe hadn't realized what a deep-founded fear it was, but the questions had been brewing inside him for too long now. He'd simply never acknowledged them.

"Monroe . . . I'm a big girl. I make my own choices, and I have to face those consequences. If something happens to me . . . it won't be your fault."

He wished her words were reassuring. But they weren't.

"I could have lost you tonight." His voice cracked.

"But you didn't. Thanks to how quickly you acted, I'm alive still."

"What if I'm not there next time you need me?"

Charlie squeezed his hand but didn't say anything.

Because there was nothing to say.

Charlie knew as well as Monroe did that one day, evil might win over good. That Charlie might lose her life as she fought for the justice she sought.

The thought pressed on his chest as he stood at her bedside waiting for news about this fake nurse.

Had she escaped? He didn't know.

But one thing was for certain.

He wasn't leaving Charlie's side.

THIRTY-FOUR

FOUR HOURS LATER, at the ripe hour of 3:30 a.m., Monroe and Charlie headed back to the ranch.

She didn't want to wait another moment after being released to go home from the hospital.

Her body was weary, but her mind was wired—despite the resounding ache in her head.

For now, she and Monroe sat beside each other with more questions than answers. As soon as that seatbelt sign went dark, Charlie took hers off and curled into a ball next to Monroe.

He wrapped his arms around her, and for a moment Charlie felt safe.

However, she knew the feeling was only temporary.

This ordeal was far from over.

"You've been here for me through a lot," she murmured into Monroe's chest.

"It's been my privilege."

Charlie knew he meant the words. Monroe truly did care about her.

She lifted her head and planted a kiss on his lips. He returned the gesture.

Before Charlie knew it, they were wrapped up in a long kiss she never wanted to end.

But she forced herself to stop so she could look him in the eyes. "I love you, Monroe."

He stared at her for a moment, and Charlie wasn't sure how he'd react.

He'd told her he'd loved her since they first met. But what if she was moving too fast and scaring him?

She didn't think he was that type of guy. But the most stable of men could be frightened away by an overeager woman.

Charlie hadn't thought about her words. She'd simply said what was on her heart.

But she knew she'd spoken the truth.

She *did* love Monroe, and she had for a long time.

Finally, after what seemed like forever, he grinned. "I love you too, Charlie Soldier."

He bent toward her and planted a soft kiss on her lips.

She remained close, her cheek touching his and

her arms wrapped around his neck as they leaned into each other.

Her heart had never felt so full—and she'd be a fool to ever walk away from someone like Monroe. Never had she felt this loved and protected.

Now that her walls had come down, the warmth that flooded her heart was something she treasured—and something she hadn't even realized she'd been missing out on.

"Do you want to hear a crazy idea?" she murmured.

"I'm always up for a crazy idea with you."

Her arms remained looped around his neck. "We should elope."

His eyebrows shot up. "What?"

"I mean . . . I don't ever want to be without you. We've known each other three years. It's not like we just started getting to know each other or something."

He didn't miss a beat before saying, "Okay."

Her eyebrows shot up this time. "Okay?"

Okay as if he was confused? Or okay as if he agreed?

She held her breath as she waited to find out.

He grinned. "Let's elope."

"You mean it?"

He nodded. "When you know it's right, you know it's right."

Charlie skimmed her fingers along his jaw. "I feel the same way. You know, Pastor Larry comes to the ranch on Sundays for our cowboy church service."

"Then he should do the ceremony. But are you sure you don't want something bigger? Grander?"

"I'm positive. I just want you and a few of our closest friends."

He grinned. "Okay then. Sunday it is."

Charlie leaned up and gave him another long kiss. Then she settled her head on Monroe's shoulder for the rest of the flight home.

———

Monroe kept replaying his conversation with Charlie.

If he ever decided to propose again, he hadn't been sure that was exactly how he saw it going.

But he wasn't complaining.

Because the woman he loved also loved him.

Now they were going to get married.

Nothing would make Monroe happier.

Although, he *would* be a little more comfortable if someone wasn't trying to kill her right now.

He bristled at the thought.

As Charlie snuggled against his shoulder, his arms tightened around her waist.

He would do whatever it took to keep her safe.

Always.

Everything he'd hoped for seemed to come true every time he looked into her eyes. Charlie completed him—and he hoped she'd say the same about him.

A couple of hours later, they finally landed.

Charlie stirred before looking up at him through her sleepy gaze. A slow smile spread across her face. "Are we back?"

"We are."

"Good. I'm tired of going back and forth to the East Coast. I just want to stay put for a while."

"I'm ready for you to be around for a while." He felt certain Amberly was also, even if the teen never admitted it.

As they taxied down the runway, Charlie's phone rang.

She squinted when she saw the number. "It's from DC."

She licked her lips before pushing the phone to her ear. She muttered several things before ending the call and turning toward him.

"It was about Bentley . . ."

"Did he know something about the note?"

"I . . . I don't know. He was in an accident on his way home from the hospital."

"What?" Monroe muttered. "Is he okay?"

"He's in the ICU, but he's stable. For now."

Monroe bristled again. "Another accident? I don't think so."

Charlie's gaze met his. "My thoughts exactly."

THIRTY-FIVE

CHARLIE LAY on the couch when she got back to the ranch and tried to let sleep find her. It was no use.

Her mind raced a million miles a minute.

She kept reflecting on everything that had happened. Being rammed by that vehicle and pushed off the road. The note she'd found. The fentanyl. The fact that Bentley was now in the hospital fighting for his life.

How far would these people go in order to keep their secrets quiet?

Charlie didn't want to find out, but she had a feeling she was going to anyway.

She turned over on the couch again and hugged her pillow to her chest.

Then her thoughts turned to Monroe, and she smiled.

They would get married on Sunday. At least, it was *something* to look forward to in these otherwise bleak circumstances.

However, she needed to tell Monroe about Amberly and the story behind her pregnancy.

Charlie sighed. She dreaded the conversation.

Why did it seem like the good and the bad parts of life always walked hand-in-hand?

As she turned over again, her phone buzzed.

She glanced at the screen and saw Ainsley had texted.

> I just found out something you're going to want to know. Can we meet in the mess hall? I'd rather talk face-to-face.

Charlie sat up on the couch. She hadn't been able to sleep anyway. So why just lie here? She might as well do something productive.

She typed back:

> Be right there.

She quickly threw a sweatshirt on and slipped her feet into her shoes. Everything else in the house was still quiet, and there was no need to wake up Monroe or Amberly to let them know where she was going. They both needed their rest.

Quietly, she slipped outside and walked through the still darkness toward the mess hall.

If Ainsley wanted to meet at this time of night, it must be important.

Ainsley had helped Charlie discover a key piece of evidence involving Jack Earl, the CEO of the media company NorthStar. He'd collected blackmail information on many key players, but it had been kept under encryption. Thankfully, Carter Winslow—Ainsley's boyfriend—had been able to break the code.

She stepped into the mess hall and flipped on the lights.

As she did, her phone buzzed again.

It was Ainsley with another text message.

> I'll be there in a few. Just getting my shoes on.

Charlie headed to her office, deciding to sit down and gather her thoughts a moment until Ainsley arrived.

But when she stepped inside and hit the light switch, the room remained dark.

Strange. The lights worked in the mess hall.

Had something come unplugged?

She started to check. But as she did, she felt a shift behind her.

She sensed she wasn't alone.

Before she could react, a deep voice filled the air. "Hello, Charlie."

———

"I bet you never thought you'd hear from me again," the unseen man crowed.

Charlie's blood went ice cold as she froze.

All she could hear was her pulse pounding in her ears.

All she could feel was her heart thumping in her chest.

All she could smell was that sickly yet familiar piney cologne.

Charlie! Snap out of it.

In the blink of an eye, she returned to reality.

She reached for her weapon.

Her stomach dropped.

She hadn't brought her pistol with her, she realized. She hadn't thought she'd need it.

A click sounded near her ear—the click of a gun being cocked. "I wouldn't do that."

The intruder already had his gun aimed at her, didn't he?

"Stay where you are," the man demanded. "Don't test me."

Charlie could barely make out his figure. He was only a shadow.

Then he stood close. Too close.

"Have you missed me?" One of his hands went to her waist as he stood behind her.

Memories from the past bombarded her until she could hardly breathe.

Memories of feeling vulnerable. Trapped. Powerless.

She never wanted to feel those ways again, and she'd worked her entire life to ensure she never did.

But the feelings all came rushing back now, as if they'd remained just below the surface all this time.

"Get your hands off me," Charlie finally said, but her voice quaked uncontrollably as she said the words.

"Why? You didn't miss me?" A teasing tone curled his voice.

"Not for one single moment." Her words came out through clenched teeth.

She started to jerk away when she felt the barrel of the gun press into her side.

"I said don't move," he growled.

Charlie had no doubt this man would pull the trigger.

He was that kind of person. The kind who liked to be in control. Who wasn't affected by the suffering of others.

"What are you doing here?" Her voice sounded bold as she asked the question.

Charlie liked to think of herself as strong.

But her past felt stronger right now.

So strong that she was having trouble moving beyond the memories that bombarded her.

She had to get a grip. Because the mental game right now was more of a struggle than anything physical would be.

"I came to see you," the man said as he shut the door behind them. "And our daughter, of course."

CHAPTER
THIRTY-SIX

THE CONTENTS of Charlie's stomach began to rise in her.

Only over her dead body would this man get anywhere close to Amberly.

But right now, Charlie was at this monster's mercy.

Even though she felt his gun pressing into her ribs, she couldn't see anything but faint shadows. Couldn't see a way to defend herself without getting killed first.

She drew in a shaky breath instead. "You should leave before someone finds you here. It won't be good for you when they do."

Her thoughts continued to race. How had this man managed to steal Ainsley's phone? It was the only thing that made sense. Otherwise, he wouldn't have been able to text her from Ainsley's number.

He'd thought of everything, hadn't he?

Even a way to get beyond the fence surrounding her ranch.

"Don't you worry about me," the man crooned. "I'm doing just fine."

"How did you get inside the gate?" Charlie had a state-of-the-art security system around this place. No one slipped past. Even if they got past the perimeter surrounding the ranch, he should have never gotten past the gate.

Her blood went even colder as reality hit her.

Unless somebody else let him inside.

But that would mean there was a mole among her staff.

She could hardly stomach that thought. She'd handpicked everyone here. Would one of them really betray her?

"So . . ." He leaned close enough that Charlie felt his breath on her ear. Smelled the sickly scent of pine.

He'd always loved that cologne.

"I see that you and Monroe have grown very close," he muttered.

"What about it?" Charlie wouldn't give him the satisfaction of an explanation.

"You know that we're all alike," the man continued. "All men—true men—like to dominate. There's no way that former football player and testosterone junkie is going to let you call the shots. You're a fool if you think that isn't true."

"Monroe is different."

The man chuckled before the sound turned into devious laughter.

"None of us are different. All men are made the same. You think he won't hurt you, but he will. You think he's going to put your needs over his own, but he won't. Men like what they like, and they don't like to be emasculated by domineering women who think they're smarter than everyone else. So if you're dreaming about your little happily ever after, you should just face the facts. It will never happen the way you want it to."

Moisture pressed against Charlie's eyes. Why was she letting him get to her? She was stronger than this.

Pull yourself together, Charlie!

"Nice try." She forced the words out, unsure if she really believed them. But she couldn't let him know that. "But this little talk isn't going to work. Not everyone is like you."

"Does he know about me?" The question had a haunting tone, almost as if he were enjoying this conversation.

Charlie tried to swallow the knot in her throat.

She could lie and deny it. But this man knew her well enough to sense when she wasn't telling the truth.

"You haven't . . ." he said after a moment of silence. "Isn't that interesting? Is that because I'm your dirty little secret?"

"You really think that's the way it went down? Because that's not the way I remember it."

The gun pressed harder into her side until she nearly yelped with pain. "You always did have a smart mouth."

Charlie sucked in another deep breath as she fought to maintain control. "Why are you here?"

"Because I need you to know that you're not safe from me, and you never will be. I could kill you right now."

"But will you?"

He chuckled. "I figure that would be a little too easy now, wouldn't it? What would be the fun in that?"

Too easy? Fun? What did that even mean?

The next moment, a cloth clamped across her mouth.

Charlie struggled against it, fought against the slightly sweet scent.

She knew what that scent was—chloroform. Knew what breathing it in would do to her.

But it was no use.

Drowsiness consumed her.

Then everything went black.

———

Monroe tossed and turned in bed.

He couldn't sleep. He had too much on his mind.

And knowing that Charlie was just in the other room did nothing to help.

But it was better if he stayed on this side of the door.

He still felt like grinning from ear to ear every time he thought about the two of them getting married.

He was the luckiest man in the whole world.

He knew that without a doubt.

Once they wrapped up this investigation, everything should be smooth sailing afterward. He knew that would be easier said than done, but they were getting closer and closer to answers.

He lay in bed several more minutes, his thoughts tossing back and forth, before finally throwing the covers off.

He needed some water. But he would stay away from Charlie as he trekked toward the kitchen.

She needed her rest.

He threw a shirt on before quietly opening the door and easing from his room. He tried to not even look at the couch where Charlie slept.

Instead, he headed toward the kitchen, grabbed a bottle of water, and then started back to his temporary room.

But this time, he couldn't resist the temptation to peek at Charlie as she slept.

He sucked in a breath when he saw the empty couch. Only a pillow and rumpled blanket were there.

Where was she?

Then he realized what had probably happened.

Charlie liked to work almost as much as he did. She'd probably gone to her office to look over some things.

Should he check on her?

He wasn't sure.

Something buzzed in his bedroom.

His phone. He'd left it charging there on the nightstand.

He quickly grabbed it and glanced at the screen. If someone was trying to get in touch with him at this time of night, there was probably an important reason.

He saw it was William Tate and pressed the phone to his ear. "What's going on?"

"I thought you'd like to know that ADPS is putting together a warrant to search the ranch."

Monroe's breath caught. "What?"

"I don't know how long it will take to get approved, but Detective Vincent is determined to get into that ranch and dig deeper." His friend talked in a whisper, as if he were afraid of being caught. "I can't talk long. But I wanted to let you know."

Monroe ended the call and pushed the phone into his pocket. Now he had no choice but to find Charlie.

They needed a backup plan, and she needed to know what was going on.

He pulled his shoes on and then quietly closed the front door behind him, locking it so Amberly would be safe inside.

Sometimes it seemed foolish to lock the doors out here on this ranch because it was so secure.

But old habits were hard to break.

He rushed to the mess hall and stepped inside.

The lights in the dining area were on, which seemed to prove his theory that Charlie was inside.

But her office looked surprisingly dark.

Tension edged between his shoulders as he started that way.

But when he reached her doorway, he saw Charlie lying on the floor . . . unconscious.

THIRTY-SEVEN

CHARLIE FELT SOMEONE SHAKE HER. Heard voices. Felt aware of the cool tile beneath her.

Where was she? What had happened?

"Charlie . . . stick with me," the deep voice said again.

Stick with him? What she really wanted was to drift back to sleep.

She moaned and kept her eyes shut.

"Charlie . . . I need you to wake up. The police are coming."

The police?

Her mind suddenly felt alert.

She jerked her eyes open, her foggy thoughts beginning to clear.

At once, all the memories hit her.

He'd been here.

At the ranch.

And he'd given her a drug so she'd pass out.

She gasped as flashbacks hit her, and she tried to scramble away from the man leering in front of her.

"Charlie . . . it's me."

Slowly, her gaze focused.

Monroe knelt beside her.

Not that man.

She nearly collapsed back onto the floor at the realization.

Before she could, Monroe's arms surrounded her. Charlie leaned into him, unable to hold back her tears.

"What happened?" he murmured as he stroked her hair.

Charlie tried to hold herself together. But it was no use. She was an emotional wreck.

She couldn't even speak.

"Let me call the doctor." Monroe reached for his phone. "I'm worried about you."

She placed her hand on his arm. "No. It's okay. I'll be fine."

She did a quick inventory of herself. Her clothes were in place. Nothing hurt.

"Charlie . . ."

Her thoughts scrambled to another realization.

"Someone got past the gate. He was just here. I don't know if he's gone . . ."

Alarm raced through his gaze. "Let me call the crew and let them know. They'll search for him."

"Amberly . . ."

"I just left her. She's okay. Your house is secure. I made sure of it."

A small measure of relief softened her tense muscles.

She started to rise, and Monroe helped her to her feet. "Listen . . . I just need to lie down a moment."

Charlie was so shaky that she couldn't think. She felt at a loss as to what she should do.

Unless she gained control of herself, she wouldn't be able to help anyone.

"You need to tell me what happened." Monroe held onto her arms as he stared her in the eye.

She blinked several times. "How did you even find me?"

"I got a call from one of my contacts with the Arizona Department of Public Safety. Detective Vincent is trying to get a warrant so he can come out here and search this place."

"What? When?" Charlie's head began to spin at the thought of it.

Then she remembered Monroe had said something about the police coming.

"They could come at any time, depending on when the judge issues the warrant," Monroe said. "What do you want me to do?"

Her thoughts continued to swirl, unable to focus.

Finally, Charlie said words she hardly ever muttered.

"I don't know, Monroe. I don't know what to do."

———

Monroe called Jesse and gave him the update. Then he took Charlie back to her house.

At her insistence, he checked Amberly's bedroom.

The girl was sound asleep, clueless that anything had happened.

Good.

He led Charlie to the couch and made sure she was seated. Then he grabbed some water for her and sat beside her.

Charlie stared at the wall as if still in shock.

"What happened, Charlie? Who did this to you?"

She said nothing.

Worry sent pulse waves through him.

As much as he wanted to figure this out, he knew his team was coming to meet him right now so they could talk about that warrant. He'd normally let

Charlie handle a situation like this, but she wasn't in the right frame of mind.

"I'll be right back, okay?" Monroe told her.

She pulled her knees to her chest and nodded.

The sight of her like this caused an ache to form in his chest. But right now he had to deal with this other situation.

He stepped outside, where several operatives waited for his update.

His gaze went to Jesse's. "Did you find anyone?"

"No one's here," Jesse said. "But the cameras went black for several minutes."

The ball in Monroe's gut tightened.

"Where's Charlie?" A knot of confusion formed on Sienna's forehead as she stood in the semi-circle that had formed around him.

"She's not feeling well." Monroe knew he should only offer as few details as possible. "Did any of you see anything strange happen tonight?"

They all shook their heads.

"Is Charlie going to be okay?" Ainsley asked.

Monroe forced himself to nod. "I hope so. I wish we could talk about that some more, but we can't right now. We have another more pressing matter we need to attend to."

He explained his phone call with William.

"So what are we going to do?" Jesse asked. "I

threw out the idea a while ago that maybe our guests could go to the lodge and stay there until this passes."

Monroe's jaw tightened. "I'm afraid that will traumatize them even more. We need to get them somewhere safe, somewhere they won't be as scared. The lodge isn't finished being built yet. There are too many dangers to the children who are staying with us."

"What do you suggest?" Mateo asked.

He exchanged a glance with Ainsley, and she nodded. She was the only other person in this group who knew about this possibility. Charlie had wanted to keep things under wraps . . . and then with the grenade and Monroe's injuries, it had gone to the back burner.

He sucked in a deep breath before starting. "Just under a month ago, Carter Winslow purchased a property not far from here just in case we ever needed to use it. I think this constitutes an emergency need to use it."

"What property are you talking about?" Ruger shifted, not bothering to hide his confusion.

"It actually happens to be the house where we busted the Geminis a few months ago."

"That place?" Mateo ran a hand through his hair.

"I didn't think I'd ever be going back there. But it's definitely big enough to house everyone."

Mateo knew all about the house's history. It wasn't pretty.

But the place would be safe from the cops.

"What about the horses?" Hudson nodded toward the stables.

"We're going to need a few people to stay here to keep an eye on them and make it look as if everything is normal. And we'll need to be careful when we wake up the guests so we don't freak them out. The situation will be tricky."

Sienna stepped forward. "We can do it."

He liked her confidence. "We'll need to gather Suzy also. And Vanessa. Take Kota but leave Chef. We'll need a few people here to look legit and not raise suspicions."

"Should we start now?" Ainsley asked.

Monroe met each of their gazes as he nodded. "Yes, there's no time to waste."

He hoped Charlie didn't mind that he'd stepped in.

And unfortunately, he couldn't help the rest of the team right now.

Because he needed to check on Charlie.

CHARLIE WAS STILL REELING as she sat on the couch.

She could still feel the man's hands on her waist. Feel his breath tickling her ear. Smell the piney scent emanating from him.

Each took her back in time.

Back to a day when she wasn't as strong as she was today.

She thought she'd overcome so many obstacles.

But maybe she'd skirted around those issues instead of truly dealing with them.

Maybe she wasn't any stronger today than she'd been back when she was fifteen.

"Charlie?" Amberly stepped out of her room and stared at her, blinking with sleepiness. "Why are people outside our place? What's going on?"

"Don't worry about it. Monroe is handling it." Her voice sounded listless, no matter how much she tried to pull herself together.

Amberly's hands fisted at her sides. She stared at her. "I'm not a baby. I know something is happening right now. Something bad, probably."

"Don't worry about it."

"Why are you shutting me out?" The words came out loud and demanding.

"I'm not trying to shut you out." Charlie ran a hand through her hair, her head pulsing even harder. "There are just some things that you aren't meant to handle. I'm trying to protect you."

"Protect me?" Amberly's nostrils flared. "Is that what you call this?"

"Amberly . . . if you could just give me a moment before you start attacking my every decision again."

"Oh, it's always all about you, isn't it?"

"That's not fair."

"What's not fair is the fact that I have to stay here at this ranch in the middle of nowhere with a mother who doesn't even love me. Maybe I'd be better off with my dad!"

Amberly stormed to her room.

As she did, Charlie buried her face.

The girl had no idea.

And that's the way she wanted to keep it . . . no matter how much it hurt.

———

Monroe stepped back inside and noted that Charlie looked as if she was in worse shape now than she'd been earlier.

He'd heard voices coming from inside and had figured that Charlie and Amberly had another falling out of sorts.

He carefully lowered himself on the cushion beside Charlie, knowing he needed to tread carefully. "We're gathering up all the residents to take to the House of Winslow."

That's what they'd decided to call the place—because that was Carter's last name.

"Good idea." She nodded, though barely.

"Do you want to take Amberly?"

"It's probably a good idea."

He placed his hand on her knee, but she jerked it away.

He furrowed his brow. "Charlie . . . I'm really worried about you. Can you please tell me what happened?"

"It's just that I've . . . I've made a lot of mistakes."

"We all have."

"Mine are bigger."

"Like what?"

She frowned and offered a terse shrug. "Like . . . thinking I could be happy with someone."

"You're talking about us?" Surprise washed through him. Was that what she was saying?

"Men are all the same, aren't they?" She continued to stare into space.

"Charlie . . . what happened to you? You don't even sound like yourself right now."

She turned toward him, and their gazes met. "Monroe, the truth is that my actions here at the ranch . . . they can destroy you. What if everyone I've hired and everyone who's believed in me goes to prison because of me?"

Was that where this was coming from? "You haven't done anything wrong."

"I've helped women acquire fake identities—driver's licenses, birth certificates, social security cards. And that's just the start of it. If the right—or wrong—people come after me, they can make me look as guilty as sin."

"Who are you? This isn't the Charlie I know."

"Maybe you don't know me at all." Her words came out just above a whisper.

"Charlie . . ." He was at a loss at what to say and

certain that whatever words left his lips would be the wrong ones.

She looked up, and her gaze met his. "There's something I need to tell you."

"You can tell me anything."

"Amberly's dad . . . his name is Brian Cox. He was married to my mother. And he's the man who was here at the ranch tonight."

CHARLIE COULDN'T BELIEVE she'd said the words aloud. She'd held them inside for so long—the revelation that Amberly was conceived out of . . . rape.

Monroe blinked. "Wait . . . Brian was here? Tonight? He's the reason I found you on the floor?"

Her throat tightened until she could hardly breathe. "He was in my office. He lured me there. He used Ainsley's phone somehow."

Monroe stood, his muscles bristling with anger. "We've got to look for him—"

"He's probably gone. He just wanted to come and send a message. To mess with my mind."

"I'm going to call Jesse and Hudson so they can search the ranch. We need to be sure."

She nodded, knowing that was a good idea.

After making the calls, Monroe sat back down slowly. But tension continued to thrum through his body with enough intensity that Charlie could practically feel it.

"What happened, Charlie?" he asked.

She pulled her knees closer to her chest. "About six months after my dad passed, Brian moved in with us. My mom . . . well, as you know, she wasn't always a faithful spouse. She blamed it on my dad's football schedule, but she was really just insecure and needed attention to make her feel worthy."

He waited for her to continue.

"From the moment I met Brian, I didn't like the way he looked at me. But my mom wouldn't listen. She was too caught up in herself. Whenever Brian became violent with her, I interjected myself so I could try to help. I ended up with black eyes and broken bones, even."

"Go on." He said the words softly and gently without any pressure.

"Finally, one night I'd had enough. I couldn't convince my mom to leave Brian. I didn't want to leave her. But I figured she loved him more than she loved me. So I packed my things. I was dating . . . Pierce at the time."

"Okay."

"But before I left, Brian charged into my room. He

was so angry and determined to teach me a lesson, to prove to me that I had no power over him . . ."

Monroe squeezed her hand. "You don't have to finish."

He clearly had a picture about what happened.

But Charlie couldn't stop now. "He . . . he assaulted me. Afterward, I told my mom what happened, but she didn't believe me. In fact, she called me a whore."

"I'm so sorry."

"I felt so lost. I went to Pierce and thought maybe I could stay with him. He was older than me and in college. I hoped I could stay in his off-campus apartment. He knew I was upset, but I didn't tell him what happened. I . . . I was too ashamed."

She drew in a shaky breath and stared at her hands in her lap.

"Three months later, I wasn't feeling well. I hadn't been for a while. I took a test and found out I was pregnant. Pierce thought the baby was his and insisted I get an abortion. I told him I couldn't do that. Then he insisted on a paternity test, and he found out the baby wasn't his. That meant the baby was . . ."

"Brian's." Monroe's jaw tightened when he said the man's name.

"Pierce was furious. I tried to tell him I'd been

assaulted, but he wouldn't listen. He said I'd cheated on him. After that, I knew I couldn't be with Pierce anymore. He'd shown me his true character, and I didn't want anything to do with him."

"So what did you do?"

"I hopped around from friend's house to friend's house. I was spiraling and making a lot of really bad decisions. I could have asked for help, but I was too proud. But I was also terrified."

"Rightfully so."

"Then one day, as I noticed my stomach getting bigger, reality hit me. I knew I couldn't keep living like I was, if not for my sake, then for my baby's. I hit rock bottom and prayed that God would show me what to do. That same day I ran into Greta while I was out shopping. She saw what a mess I was and invited me to stay at her house. I swallowed my pride and accepted."

"Charlie . . . I'm so sorry. I didn't know." Monroe squeezed her hand.

"You're the only other person I've told besides Greta and Wallace. Otherwise, I've kept the story to myself."

"Did you ever think about pressing charges against Brian?"

"I was worried that news about what had happened would leak to the press if I did. My family was already tabloid fodder. I had visions of my assault ending up as front-page news. I couldn't handle the possibility. So I kept it quiet."

Monroe pulled her into a hug, but Charlie stiffened.

She wanted nothing more than to melt into his arms.

But the stakes . . . they were higher than she ever anticipated. And the people she loved the most were the ones who'd pay the price.

She loved Monroe too much to let that happen.

"I meant what I said earlier, Monroe." Her gaze locked with his. "I stand behind everything I've done here at the ranch. But I can't let you take the fall for me. They're going to paint everyone who works for me as criminals instead of heroes."

"I'll be by your side the whole time."

"I can't let you do this." She swung her head back and forth.

"Charlie . . ."

They stared at each other in a silent standoff.

A knock at the door broke the moment.

Monroe stood, not hiding his hesitation. "I better get that."

She nodded, knowing he should.

He opened the door, and Jesse stood outside, his

expression pensive. "We didn't find anyone. We searched everywhere. He must have gotten away."

"But everyone here is accounted for?" Monroe asked.

"Yes, they are." Jesse shifted. "The guys are about to leave. Do you want them to take Amberly to the House of Winslow?"

Monroe looked back at Charlie.

She thought about his question a moment before nodding. "It's probably better if she's there. But I'll stay behind. It will be suspicious if I'm not here when the police show up."

"Do you want me to stay or go?" Jesse asked.

"You and Sienna stay," Charlie said. "A married couple will also seem less suspicious."

"Got it."

"I'll get Amberly for you." Monroe strolled across the floor to her room, knocked, then opened the door a crack. "Amberly, we need you to go with the guys to somewhere a little safer."

But there was no answer.

He opened the door farther. "Amberly?"

Charlie jumped to her feet and hurried into the room, flipping the light on.

But the room was empty.

Amberly was gone.

—————

Monroe was worried about Charlie. Really worried.

But right now, he needed to figure out where Amberly had gone. Especially considering everything that had transpired over the last hour.

Amberly had been arguing with Charlie only twenty minutes ago.

Her bedroom window had been left open.

Had someone slipped inside? Or had she slipped outside?

Monroe paced toward the door. "I'm going to go see if Jonathan has seen her."

"I'll go too."

He raised his hand and gently stopped her in her tracks. "You should stay here and get yourself together first. I'll be back with the update, though. Okay?"

He thought for sure that Charlie would argue with him. But she didn't.

Instead, she nodded. "O . . . okay then."

As he hurried from the house, he saw Mateo and quickly barked out instructions. "I need you to stay outside Charlie's place and keep an eye on it for a few minutes. Okay?"

A look of confusion crossed his face. "Did I miss something?"

"I can't give details right now. But Amberly is missing, and I need to find her. Speaking of which, have you seen Jonathan?"

"The last time I saw him was probably thirty minutes ago. He was in the bunkhouse."

Monroe rushed that way.

But even as he approached the building, he noticed that Jonathan's truck wasn't parked behind the bunkhouse anymore.

Had he taken off with Amberly?

He tried to reserve judgment.

But as he stepped inside the bunkhouse, he realized the place was empty.

So was Jonathan's bed and the small dresser beside it. He must have packed all his belongings and put them in the truck.

Then he'd taken off with Amberly.

Monroe guessed that Amberly was probably upset after her fight with Charlie. She'd decided to act out and leave rather than stay here.

If they'd left twenty minutes ago, they could be a good distance from this ranch by now. Their security system should have alerted them—but Amberly was a smart girl. She listened more than people gave her credit for. He'd bet she knew how to get around their sensors.

Either way, he and Charlie didn't have any time

to waste.

He rushed back to Charlie's place and hurried inside.

She stood with her arms crossed near the door as if waiting for him. She jerked her head up as he closed the door behind him.

"Well?" Hope saturated her voice.

"Jonathan's gone. I can only assume he and Amberly left together."

She pressed her eyes closed as if this was one more burden she couldn't carry. "I knew I should have fired him."

"You can't think about that now. I'm going to take the Jeep and see if I can find them."

"Aren't you on pain meds? Can you drive?"

"I didn't take them this morning." He nodded toward the door. "I know you're going to want to come with me, so let's go."

Almost as if in a trance, Charlie followed him outside.

He paused long enough to tell Mateo, "We've got to go look for Amberly and Jonathan. Keep an eye on things here."

"Will do. A bunch of people just left for the House of Winslow."

"Perfect."

Monroe took off toward a garage where they kept

some of their vehicles.

He grabbed the keys and jumped into one of their Jeeps.

Wasting no time, Charlie climbed into the seat beside him and pulled on her seatbelt.

He wasn't used to seeing her so quiet and withdrawn. It worried him.

And if they didn't find Amberly . . . he didn't know what Charlie would do.

CHAPTER
FORTY

CHARLIE STILL COULDN'T BELIEVE Amberly was gone. That she'd left with Jonathan. That she'd run away before they could talk again.

As they started away from the property, she glanced at Monroe. "Do you think Jonathan's the mole?"

"He could be."

"He could have let Brian inside. And if Jonathan is the mole, and Amberly has gone with him . . . she's in serious trouble." Some of her focus slowly returned as her shock from seeing Brian wore off.

But she still wasn't a hundred percent yet.

"Let's not jump to any conclusions," Monroe reminded her.

They started across the landscape, the Jeep's headlights illuminating the ground in front of them.

"There's a chance we're not going to catch up with them." Charlie reached for the bar above her as they bounced along the uneven landscape. The roads near the ranch were dirt and not maintained by the county.

"Let's just stay positive."

"I shouldn't have kept her in the dark. At least, not about the police coming."

"You didn't do the wrong thing," Monroe told her. "She's a teen. There are some burdens she shouldn't have to carry."

"I know, but she's so much like me, and this is *exactly* what I would've done at her age. I should've known better."

Monroe didn't say anything. His hand simply covered her knee.

Charlie found so much comfort in his touch, though she knew she should pull away.

The reality of their situation had become all too clear within the past hour.

She wasn't the type who'd ever be able to marry. She'd made too many mistakes and carried too much baggage.

She had the potential to destroy Monroe's life, and she couldn't live with herself if she ever did that. Her headstrong attitude and gung ho commitment to help people could wreck the innocent lives of people who'd come on board with her.

Her happiness with Monroe had only lasted a moment, but perhaps that was too long. She'd had a taste of just how good it could be—which made her heart ache even stronger.

"Monroe . . ." Something caught her eye in the distance, and she pointed to it. "That almost looks like Jonathan's truck up there."

But it wasn't moving. The vehicle had stopped on the side of the road.

"Let's go check it out." Monroe pressed the accelerator harder.

Charlie's thoughts raced. Why would Jonathan have stopped in the middle of the desert?

She knew the answer.

He wouldn't have by his own choice.

Maybe—just maybe—the truck had broken down and that's why it sat there.

But Charlie had a feeling there was more to it than that.

Monroe stopped and threw the Jeep into Park. Then he grabbed his gun and approached the truck.

Charlie followed behind him.

When he opened the door, he spotted Jonathan. The teen cradled his head in his arms as he bent over in what had to be an uncomfortable position across the bench seat.

"Where's Amberly?" Monroe demanded.

Jonathan slowly pulled his eyes open. He unwound from his fetal position when he saw Monroe. "I'm . . . sorry."

"Sorry about what?" Charlie's voice hardened as she anticipated what he'd say.

"A car ran us off the road. Then two men got inside. They grabbed Amberly. I tried to stop them, but I couldn't."

"They took her?" Charlie's voice cracked.

"I promise, I did what I could to stop them. But they hit me on the head, and I passed out. Just before they knocked me out . . . they said if the police found out, Amberly was as good as dead."

Charlie and Monroe exchanged a glance.

Before she could fully comprehend what was happening, the flash of red and blue lights in the distance caught her eye.

The police were on their way.

Everything had just gotten a lot more complicated.

———

Monroe felt his jaw tighten as he stared at Jonathan and listened to his explanation.

One thing was clear: They didn't have any time to waste.

Amberly had been abducted.

"We need to get you back to the ranch," Monroe nodded to the Jeep. "Get in. Now."

Jonathan didn't argue.

Monroe put the teen in the back of the Jeep and then raced back toward the ranch, toward the back entrance where the police wouldn't see them.

As he did, his thoughts spun.

But what exactly was someone planning on doing with Amberly?

Part of him didn't want to know the answer to that question. He couldn't bear to think about it. He'd seen and heard some terrible things during his time at the ranch.

No one should have to suffer at the hands of evil men. No one.

They reached the ranch, and he pulled the Jeep behind the bunkhouse. Then he turned to Jonathan.

"I need you to go get cleaned up," Monroe said. "The police are going to be here any moment, and you need to tell them that you're a ranch hand here. If you so much as make any indication that there's anything else going on, you're going to have to deal with me personally. Understand?"

The teen's eyes widened as he nodded. "Understood." He swallowed hard. "Should I tell them about Amberly?"

"No!" Charlie said the word quickly. "If the police get involved, she could die. I have a feeling some of these officers are in the pockets of the men who took her. We can't risk it."

Monroe nodded. The choice was a hard one, but he agreed with her.

Jonathan rushed inside the bunkhouse.

Monroe didn't think they would have any problems with him complying, but he couldn't be certain.

This was still going to be a precarious situation.

Just as he and Charlie stepped toward the mess hall, the police arrived at the gate.

Six cars had come this time.

The cops had really pulled out all the stops.

"Just keep a cool head," he reminded Charlie as she stared at the scene.

It didn't feel right to have to tell her that. She was usually so in control.

Monroe only prayed he'd be there for her the way she needed right now.

Charlie had helped so many people.

Now it was time for everyone to help her.

CHARLIE DREW in a deep breath and tried to pull herself together.

She didn't have much other choice at the moment. She had to get through this so she could find Amberly.

Hearing that her daughter had been abducted had been like ice water being poured over her head. She'd snapped from her stupor in an instant.

She strode toward the gate with Monroe and spotted Detective Vincent and several of his officers standing on the other side.

She eyed him coolly. "Detective . . . I wasn't expecting to see you here again so soon."

He scowled and gave her a knowing look. "I wasn't expecting you to be awake at this time of night."

"So you're saying you wanted to surprise us?"

"I'm just saying that most people are sleeping at three a.m."

She shrugged. "What can I say? I'm an early riser. It's how I get things done."

He held up a paper. "We have a warrant to search this property."

She swallowed hard before calmly asking, "For what?"

She prayed her guys had managed to get all the women and children away from here in time. She thought they had, but it hadn't been confirmed yet.

She prayed none of her guys had run into the cops on their way to the House of Winslow.

"According to the warrant, we can search your guest cabins and talk to anyone here to see if they know anything about a potential human trafficking scheme connected with this ranch."

She stared at him a moment before nodding curtly. "Very well. I hate for you to wake up my guests for an error like this. But if it'll make you feel better."

Charlie punched in a code on the numeric pad by the gate, and it swung open.

Detective Vincent and his officers flooded inside.

She and Monroe remained at the center of the

property, at the intersection of all the buildings, and waited as the cops spread like ants at a picnic.

She wanted to get out there and search for Amberly.

But she knew it wouldn't do any good.

Those guys had taken her for a purpose, and they had enough of a head start that there was no way Charlie could find her daughter right now.

Instead, Charlie was at the mercy of the men who'd taken Amberly.

She watched as an officer stopped at one of the guest cabins and knocked.

No one answered.

Then he went to a second cabin. This time, the door opened.

Charlie watched as a sleepy-looking Jesse and Sienna answered.

Good.

It would be suspicious if all the guests were gone. But if Charlie's operatives could act as if they were the guests, then maybe they could throw the police off their scent for now.

But until these people were off Charlie's property, apprehension would continue to thrum inside her.

———

Monroe was impressed at how quickly Charlie had pulled herself together.

Just in the nick of time.

She appeared as cool as a cucumber as she stood beside him watching everything transpire. If she'd been in her stoic state, Detective Vincent would have definitely asked questions—which could lead them to more trouble.

He was not only impressed with Charlie, but he was impressed with the rest of the crew here as well.

They'd managed to pull this off without a hitch.

As Detective Vincent stormed back over to them, Monroe saw the irritation in his gaze.

The man had come here to find something specific, and he hadn't.

"We went through your office." He narrowed his eyes as he studied Charlie's face. "Where are your files?"

"I don't keep a lot of files," Charlie said. "Unless you're talking about the horses' immunization records. I can probably find those for you if you didn't see them yourself."

"I bet you could . . ." He rubbed his jaw. "We're taking your computer."

"That's fine. I have nothing to hide."

Monroe knew that Charlie kept everything on a hidden backup drive. There was no way the cops had found that, which was the only reason she could look so calm right now.

The only thing that made Monroe nervous were the fake driver's licenses, birth certificates, and social security cards they had on hand.

But they were careful with them and had stashed them in a secret compartment, hidden in the floor beneath Charlie's desk. Only he and Charlie knew where they were kept—or about the secret compartment at all.

"I'm not finished with you yet." Vincent glared at Charlie.

"It's like I said, I have nothing to hide."

"Then why didn't you let us search the premises the first time we came?" He watched her carefully.

"I may not have anything to hide, but I'm not stupid either. I know the way these things work. And I can see when someone's on a mission and already has their mind made up. I'll fight to maintain my innocence. I promise you that."

Vincent gave Charlie another glare before motioning for his guys to head out.

But not without promising they'd be back.

CHARLIE LET out a breath of relief as the cops left.

That had been close.

Too close.

As soon as they were out of sight, Monroe gathered Jesse, Sienna, Hudson, Teagan, and Chef at the center of the property to talk.

Jesse held out his hand and showed them some kind of electronic device that had been smashed. "The cops left several bugs."

Charlie's stomach clinched with more irritation. "Of course, they did. We're going to need to search this place and make sure we find every one of them. Look for cameras also."

"We can do that." Hudson shifted. "What exactly is going on?"

Charlie drew in a breath, hating the fact she had

to have this conversation. But she couldn't keep everyone in the dark.

"Someone is determined to destroy me," she started. "Now they have Amberly."

Sienna gasped. "What?"

Charlie nodded. "She and Jonathan tried to run away, but they were stopped. Amberly was taken."

"We need to find her," Hudson said.

"I know." Charlie swallowed hard before continuing. "But whoever has her is long gone by now. They said they would be in touch. But there's one more thing I need to address. Someone here at the ranch is a mole."

"What?" Jesse stared at her as if he hadn't heard correctly.

Charlie's gaze slipped to the newest person to enter their circle.

Jonathan.

She wasn't sure if she wanted him here or not.

But she knew he hadn't beaten himself up. Someone had gotten to him earlier and done a number on him.

"This evening, someone used Ainsley's phone and sent me a message that made it appear as if it was from her," Charlie explained.

"How did they do that?" Alarm filled Sienna's voice.

"My guess is that this person was able to clone her phone number. Certain technology will allow you to do that. Anyway, the text asked me to meet in the mess hall. But when I got there, it wasn't Ainsley waiting for me. It was a man named Brian Cox."

"Who is Brian Cox?" Jesse's forehead wrinkled with confusion.

Charlie held back a frown at the mere mention of the man. "Brian is the man that my mother married after my dad died. He was abusive and evil, to say the least."

"What was he doing here?" Sienna asked.

"Intimidating me," Charlie said. "But that's not my main concern right now. I need to know how he got in. Someone had to let him through the gates."

"You know none of us would do that," Hudson said.

"I don't want to believe anyone I've hired would do that. But I'd be naive to turn a blind eye to this. There's no way this guy got inside without help." She stared into the faces of everyone around her. "We need to figure out who it was."

Jonathan raised his hands as he noticed everyone looking at him. "It wasn't me. I promise."

"Then who else would have done it?" Monroe asked.

No one said anything.

"Okay, you all know what you need to do." Charlie turned back to her crew. "Look for any listening devices, cameras, or any other surprises the cops may have left for us. They all need to be wiped from this ranch. In the meantime, I'm going to check in with everyone at the House of Winslow to make sure that they're okay."

Just as she said those words, her phone buzzed.

She glanced at the screen and saw an unknown number.

But she had a feeling she knew exactly who it was.

———

Charlie's hands trembled as she answered the FaceTime call. She didn't even bother to step away from the group.

They could know the truth.

Brian had already devastated her. He couldn't hurt her any more deeply.

A man wearing a black mask filled the screen. "I hate that I had to get your attention this way."

Did Charlie recognize that voice? She wasn't sure.

It could be Brian . . . but she didn't think so.

"You need to let her go," Charlie said. "She has nothing to do with this."

"We know that. But she has everything to do with *you*."

Her muscles went rigid. "What do you want from me?"

"We're getting to that. Instructions will be coming to you soon. You need to listen to them carefully, and don't tell the police. We will kill her if you do."

And they most likely had contacts within the department. She knew the threat was reliable.

"I need to see Amberly," Charlie said. "I need to know that she's alive and unharmed."

"We figured you'd ask that." The man turned the camera until Amberly filled the screen. She sat in the corner of a dark room with fabric tied across her mouth.

The look in her eyes was pure terror.

Charlie swallowed back a cry at the sight of her. Instead, she said, "Amberly, I'm going to find you!"

The camera jerked back to the masked man. "That's enough. Wait for our instructions."

The call ended.

Charlie gripped the phone so tightly she felt as if it might burst. Then she glanced at the crew around her.

It took every ounce of her strength to hold herself together.

But she was the leader of this group. She couldn't let them down.

Her dad had once said leadership happens when you don't give up.

She needed to make him proud right now.

FORTY-THREE

"YOU MIGHT WANT to wait before going to the House of Winslow." Hudson nodded to something in the distance.

She glanced to the other side of the fence and barely made out the vehicle parked in the distance.

Vincent had stationed one of his guys outside the ranch to keep an eye on them. She shouldn't be surprised.

"Needless to say, we all need to be careful using our phones as well," Monroe said. "There's a good chance the cops could be listening in on our conversations, especially if Vincent was convincing enough when he talked to that judge."

Charlie nodded. "He's right. We all need to be careful. I have a burner phone in my office. I can get it and call over to the house to make sure everyone's okay there. I don't believe the police know we took everyone there, but I'd like to confirm."

They all split up so they could do their tasks.

Monroe came with Charlie as she headed to her office. But there was no way she was going to have any conversations in here. Not when there was a chance that something could be overheard.

Monroe ran a scanner over everything.

He found a bug and two cameras and smashed them.

Once Charlie was sure the area was safe, she shoved her desk aside and found the hidden compartment in her floor.

Relief swept through her when she opened it.

Everything appeared to still be in place.

She grabbed one of the burner phones, and she and Monroe walked outside to the pasture—nothing was around them out here.

Pausing, she dialed Hayes' number.

He answered right away.

"It's Charlie," she started. "This is my new number—for now. How's everything going?"

"All the women are settled in and doing okay. What's going on there?"

She gave him a quick update.

"I don't like the way that sounds." Hayes' voice cracked with tension.

"We don't either. The police are watching us right now, so no one can go to the House of Winslow, nor can anyone come back to the ranch. I need you to keep everyone in place. Understand?"

"Yes, of course."

"I'm also afraid that those guys could be listening to our phone conversations—that's why I'm using a burner. I called you specifically because you're one of our newest hires, and I doubt anyone knows you're even working here. But tell everyone else to be careful about their phone calls."

"Will do."

She ended the call and turned to Monroe. She saw the questions in his gaze and hated the fact that she was the one who put those doubts there.

But this wasn't the time to talk about their relationship, and certainly he knew that also.

Before she could say anything, her phone—her old phone—buzzed again.

She glanced at the screen and saw a text from the same unknown number as before.

There was a good chance the police were monitoring this line. That they'd seen the earlier FaceTime call.

But she couldn't worry about that right now.

This time, the message contained a time and the

place to meet—an abandoned gas station in the middle of nowhere.

She only had an hour to get there and, based on what she knew about the location, it was at least sixty minutes away.

That wouldn't give her much time to plan anything in advance.

She was certain these guys had arranged it that way.

———

Charlie called a meeting behind the stables.

First, she scanned the area and didn't see anyone watching nearby. She'd even had Jesse pull out his night vision goggles to check for anyone doing a stakeout. He hadn't seen anyone.

Everything they did right now had to be done with extra caution.

And she didn't have much time to pull this together.

She watched as Jonathan approached them. But this time, he seemed to have a new purpose in his gaze.

"I found Amberly's phone." He held the device up. "She must have dropped it before we left."

"What about it?" Charlie asked.

"I wasn't trying to be nosy, but I was concerned. She told me her code to unlock it, so I was able to open it. She's been texting back and forth with someone for the past couple of days."

Charlie took the phone from him. "Who?"

"He never gave his name. But he said he was coming here tonight and that he wanted to visit you." Jonathan paused. "I hate to say it, but I think Amberly is the one who let him inside the ranch."

Charlie felt the breath leave her lungs.

Brian had gotten to Amberly. He'd used their daughter as a part of his scheme.

Anger filled her blood like lava flowing from a volcano.

She turned to the group, her determination strengthened more and more by the minute. "We can talk about this more later. Right now, I need a plan."

"The location they gave you . . ." Hudson said. "You don't have much time to get there. There's nothing else around this old gas station. If we try to follow you there and hide in the shadows, they'll still see us."

No doubt these guys had planned it that way.

"You could wear a wire," Sienna suggested.

"They'll find it. They're not stupid."

"You can't go alone." Monroe's voice cut through the somber atmosphere.

Charlie's gaze met with his. "They'll kill Amberly if I don't."

"There has to be another way."

"I wish there were."

"So, what are you suggesting?" Monroe took a step closer.

"That I go in alone—but with a plan."

"What kind of plan are you thinking of?" Caution edged Hudson's voice.

Her gaze met the eyes of everyone around her. "That's what I wanted to talk to you about."

FORTY-FOUR

MONROE DIDN'T LIKE any of this.

He wasn't comfortable with the plan.

Only a few minutes had passed since they'd decided on their strategy. And now, in what felt like the blink of an eye, Charlie had climbed into her Hummer, ready to leave.

He needed more time with her. More time to think through this situation.

But they didn't have time.

He lingered near her door, trying to find the right words.

He wished he could go to this gas station instead of Charlie.

But he knew that would never work out.

Monroe also couldn't go with her.

He knew these guys would check her vehicle.

Even if he tried to stash himself inside somewhere, they would find him. They wouldn't hesitate to kill him when they did.

But now, Charlie needed to get going.

He paused at her door, knowing that time was of the essence.

"I know what you're thinking." Charlie stared at him from behind the wheel.

Monroe shifted as he leaned against the vehicle. "You do?"

"But you're better off without me, Monroe."

His throat tightened. "I think that's for me to decide."

She shook her head, all light gone from her gaze. "You'll realize it one day."

"No, I won't. You're going to come back to me, and we're going to talk this through. Promise me." His gaze locked with hers.

Charlie stared at him, unknown emotions saturating her gaze before she finally nodded. "I'll do my best."

She gave him one last lingering look before slamming the door.

Monroe backed up as the engine started. He knew they didn't have any more time. They'd already taken too much.

But he wanted nothing more than to reach into the vehicle. To give her a hug and a kiss.

Because part of him feared this might be the last time he saw her alive.

Emotion clogged his throat.

He didn't want to think like that.

But he knew the reality—and the danger—of the situation.

Nothing about it was ideal.

He only hoped and prayed that the plan they came up with worked and that Charlie would be safe.

———

Charlie's heart raced as she headed down the dirt road, going a good twenty miles over the speed limit. But there was no one out here.

She'd managed to get around the officer stationed near the ranch—thank goodness.

She'd left out a back entrance, keeping her headlights off. Since then, she'd been keeping her eyes open for anyone who might appear behind her.

No one tailed her.

Her thoughts raced with every rotation of her tires.

Her contemplation stopped on the name Lothario.

Why did it feel as if a memory wanted her attention?

Something was niggling at her. But what?

She wasn't sure. The name hadn't seemed that significant when Mrs. Creighton said it.

But Lothario was a character who was known for being a womanizer.

So whoever was leading this organization—this nameless, faceless Lothario guy—was probably someone who thought he was a real catch.

Charlie had a feeling he was someone she might have even crossed paths with before. With all the connections between these crimes and her life, the reasoning seemed plausible.

What if someone had planted himself in her life to keep an eye on her after her father's death?

She shivered at the thought of it.

There had to be a connection somewhere.

It would come to her . . . she only hoped that didn't happen too late.

Finally, she spotted the gas station in the distance.

The place was a remnant of times past—now dilapidated and rusty, though it had once been an oasis for weary travelers. Four old-fashioned pumps stood out front of the square store, and a faded sign reading "Sparky's" hung atop the building.

The building appeared deserted, but she knew that it wasn't.

She stopped near the old gas pumps and climbed out. A cool wind swept around her as she stood there.

Instantly, men in black emerged from the shadows and surrounded her.

She raised her hands in the air, knowing there was no need to fight them.

"Search the vehicle," one of the men said.

The rest of them did as ordered.

"It's clear," another man said.

"Be thorough. Don't forget, she's smart." The man almost sounded bitter as he said the words.

"You hiding anything from us, lady?" One of the men patted her down for any wires. "There's nothing."

"Take her earrings," the guy in charge said. "She's the type who'd think of putting trackers in there. We don't want anything to get past us."

The way this guy talked, he seemed to think he knew her.

But he didn't.

None of these men knew what she was capable of.

The man practically ripped the diamond earrings

from her ears. He tossed them on the ground and stomped on them with an extra dose of vengeance.

They didn't smash. They were real diamonds.

Charlie continued to stand there, arms still raised as she contemplated what to do next. "Happy now?"

The man stepped closer. "Not yet."

She stared at the man, refusing to even blink. "Who are you?"

"It doesn't matter to you since you're never going to see the light of day again. But since you asked . . ."

The man ripped off his mask and grinned. "Did you miss me?"

"BRIAN?" Charlie could hardly believe her eyes.

She'd known how evil and depraved Brian was.

But he'd gone as far as to take Amberly?

Was he involved in the hotel bombing? The one who'd ultimately killed her dad?

How was it possible that he had that kind of power? He'd worked for a senator, so he rubbed elbows with some powerful people, but . . .

His grin widened. "I married your mom because I knew someone needed to keep an eye on the situation. It was the perfect plan, really."

"You're the one controlling senators and world leaders?" Her stepfather? Really?

She still couldn't believe it.

"Why so surprised? Don't you know legislative aides carry all the power in Washington?" He chuckled. "We always say that as a joke, but it's kind of true. No one in DC thought I was keeping track of what they were doing. Who they were meeting with. Who they talked to. I had dirt on *everybody*. And I knew what motivated these guys. And how to get exactly what I wanted."

"So you've been the puppet master this whole time." She shook her head as disgust filled her. "I guess I shouldn't be surprised."

Another memory hit her—the one that had been trying to surface.

Lothario.

That was the password Brian had used on the family computer. Charlie had watched him type it once.

She'd wanted to know what he was doing online and had figured it was gambling.

Not long after that—before Charlie could fully investigate—was when she'd left home. She'd forgotten about it as other worries were at the forefront of her mind.

Her thoughts still reeled as facts clicked into place.

She'd have to sort through all those revelations later.

She turned back to Brian. "Where is Amberly?"

"She's not here."

"Where is she?"

He shrugged as if he enjoyed having the upper hand—because, no doubt, he did. "Don't worry. You'll see her soon. I'm going to take you to her."

Charlie wanted to believe him. She really did. But she wouldn't relax until she was with her daughter again. Until she knew if she was safe.

A new sound filled the air in the distance.

A helicopter cut through the air, coming toward them.

Charlie's lungs tightened.

Her ride was here.

Once Brian put her inside that copter, he could take her anywhere.

Far away from anyone that could help her.

The chances she'd survive this were growing slimmer and slimmer.

She prayed her backup plan worked.

———

Monroe remained a safe distance from the gas station so he couldn't be seen. He'd found a small rock formation to hide behind. Jesse had come with him— but they were just here as a precaution.

Charlie had been clear that they shouldn't interfere.

Yet he was too far away to be comfortable. He wanted to be there right beside Charlie.

No, he wanted to be *in front* of her. Shielding her.

"What . . . ?" Jesse muttered as a new sound filled the air.

A helicopter appeared in the distance.

Monroe's stomach clenched. "Of course . . ."

This was a getaway vehicle—something they wouldn't be able to catch up with.

He wanted to rush to Charlie's rescue. To whisk her away.

But she'd never forgive him if he did.

Instead, he remained behind the rock formation.

No doubt that helicopter would take Charlie to Amberly.

"I'm going to call Ghost," Monroe muttered. "He can help us track this copter."

"We only have seventy-two hours to find her before . . ."

Monroe nodded.

He knew how their plan would work. He knew the stakes. The limitations.

But inside he feared he'd never see Charlie again.

He felt as if he still had a fighting chance with her.

But not if she didn't make it out of this alive.

CHAPTER
FORTY-SIX

CHARLIE'S HEAD swirled as the doors slammed shut and the copter took off.

The aircraft was nice—complete with leather seats and soundproofing. The normally loud noises of the engine and rotors were surprisingly muted, and she didn't need to wear a headset.

She glanced at Brian as the ground disappeared beneath them. "Where are you taking me?"

"Mexico. We have a nice little island there waiting for you."

An island? Charlie swallowed hard.

An island could make things more complicated.

"Is that where Amberly is?" she asked.

"It is. I'm a man of my word, in case you haven't noticed," he said above the steady thumping of the blades.

Charlie hadn't noticed that. In fact, she'd observed the opposite.

This man was evil and delusional.

"What are you going to do once we get there?" Charlie was determined to get as much information from him as she could.

If only she could have worn a wire—if there was a way of transmitting this information back to her guys. But there hadn't been any options for that.

Brian rubbed his jaw as if debating what to say. "I thought killing you might be the best way to keep you silent. But then I realized just how valuable you are."

He lifted a piece of her hair, twirling it around his finger.

Disgust roiled in Charlie's stomach, and she pulled away.

"You're going to make Amberly and me part of your industry, aren't you?" She said the word *industry* with disdain.

He grinned. "*Now* you're catching on. Whatever I can do to make a buck or two. How did you think I got so rich? By being a nice guy?"

"Using your own daughter for financial gain? You're disgusting."

He shrugged. "You used to like me."

"I've *never* liked you." She didn't bother to hold back.

"Your mom thought you did."

Charlie wanted to reach over and smack the man. But she didn't.

"Did you tell Amberly who you are?" She held her breath as she waited for his answer.

His smile widened. "I thought it would be more fun if I told her in front of you."

"You're a sorry excuse for a human being."

He scowled. "I may be, but I *am* filthy rich. Are you aware that no one knows who I am? I can do whatever I want, to whomever I want, whenever I want. Only you and a few of my most trusted men can identify me. I plan on keeping it that way."

"You were the one who planned the whole bombing down in Florida, weren't you? You took down an entire hotel full of innocent people just to keep your secret quiet."

He clucked his tongue. "Didn't you always say there's a reason for everything? The men under my thumb were panicking. They were going to start making mistakes. I'd be found out, and I couldn't let that happen."

Charlie's thoughts raced. How would she get out of this situation?

She hadn't counted on a helicopter showing up. Or being taken to an island. Or another country.

She'd always thought dying was the worst possible outcome of any given situation.

But now she had to consider that the people in this organization might actually try to sell her. To sell Amberly.

Which would be an entirely different kind of death.

A much more painful and drawn out one.

———

A few hours later, the helicopter landed in the darkness. Only a few lights twinkled in the distance and, Charlie couldn't be sure, but she thought she saw some palm trees swaying in the breeze.

"Welcome to your new home." Brian grinned at her before nodding to the two guys beside her.

One of them opened the door while the other one grabbed her arm. She let out a cry at the man's grip.

"We don't want her bruised," Brian muttered.

The man's fingers didn't loosen.

Instead, he led her from the helicopter toward a massive estate in the distance.

Charlie paused a moment as she sucked in the sight of it.

The sprawling building looked Mediterranean with its arches and sand-swept stucco. A huge fountain flowed in an alcove near the front door, and a rock path led toward the entry. Statues were placed around the property, and the lush grass indicated an expensive landscaping design.

Despite how beautiful the building was, Charlie couldn't shake the sense that terrible things had happened here.

She swallowed hard.

There was a good chance that more terrible things would happen.

But she'd do everything in her power to stop it.

"Keep moving," the man beside her grumbled, tugging at her arm again.

He walked so fast that he nearly dragged her inside.

She glanced around the space, trying to soak in every detail she could. She noted anything that could help later. The more sense of the layout of this area, the better. She needed to know about possible escape routes. Possible hideouts. Possible weapons.

"Where's my daughter?" Her voice trembled as she glanced at the men.

She wasn't sure where Brian had gone. But he wasn't with them.

However, she spotted another armed guard pacing the perimeter of this place.

How many were here?

"Stop asking questions," the man muttered as he looked at her with contempt.

Charlie stood her ground. "I want to see Amberly."

"I said be quiet." He glared at her.

A moment of panic fluttered through Charlie.

What if Amberly wasn't here? What if she'd come all this way for nothing?

FORTY-SEVEN

MONROE LOOKED at Jesse and Hudson as they gathered in the conference room at Vanishing Ranch. "Do we have a location yet?"

"I'm working on it." Sienna typed something else into her computer, her expression tense.

He didn't want to put more pressure on her, but they only had a limited amount of time for their plan to work.

"I've got something!" Sienna's voice rose with excitement. "It looks like she's in . . . Mexico."

"Mexico?" Monroe repeated. "Where in Mexico?"

She stared at the screen. "On an island off the west coast."

"See what you can find out about it," Monroe continued before glancing at Hudson. "You were a

SEAL. You know best how to plan covert rescue operations. We're going to need to come up with something—and fast."

"I'm on it." Hudson nodded.

"Okay, from what I can tell, this is a private island. It used to be owned by some TV producer. It's pretty isolated, which makes it the perfect place for people who want to do things in secret. There appear to be four buildings on the island. A main house, which is ten thousand square feet, a small guesthouse, a garage, and some other type of outbuilding."

"How far is it from the coast?" Monroe's jaw thumped.

"About two miles, but the coastline is rocky." Sienna typed something else onto the screen. "The nearest harbor is four miles away."

"Four nautical miles will be challenging," Hudson said. "How's the weather? That will affect how we proceed."

"Right now, it's clear. It looks like the skies will be clear for the next twenty-four hours, at least. Then there's a system moving across the Pacific that will bring winds and rain."

"Another reminder that time isn't on our side right now." Monroe stopped pacing and glanced at the team members around him. "This could be dangerous."

"We know." Jesse nodded.

"It could cost us everything," Monroe continued.

"Charlie would do it for us," Sienna said.

"She would. And she wouldn't bat an eye," Monroe said. "So, let's get our team together and go rescue Charlie and Amberly. We don't have time to waste."

***

"Make yourself comfortable." Brian strode into the room with an amber-colored liquid in his glass. He looked as if he owned the world.

He probably thought he did.

"Where's Amberly?" she demanded as she jerked away from her captor's grasp.

He started to grab her again when Brian shook his head at him, indicating the man could let go. "There's nowhere for her to run here. I'll take care of her."

The guard stepped away, and Charlie's lungs loosened—but barely.

"Where's Amberly?" Charlie shot lasers at Brian with her gaze.

"She's somewhere safe."

"I want to see her."

"Do I need to remind you that you're not the one calling the shots here?"

She stepped closer, anger burning through her veins. "She's your daughter. How could you do this to her?"

"How could you not tell me I had a daughter?"

"Because I didn't want her to know that her father was a monster!"

Brian's smile slipped, and he took another sip of his drink. "So feisty. I've always admired how strong you were. I could see that strength in your gaze from the moment we met."

"You mean, back when you were in your mid-thirties, and I was just a teen?" Contempt dripped from her voice.

He remained unfazed. "Let's face it, you were much more mature than most of the girls your age."

Some of Charlie's anxiety turned into anger. "Why am I here?"

His grin returned and made it clear he was enjoying this entirely too much. "I have big plans for you. Women who are this beautiful and feisty bring in a certain kind of client."

Disgust roiled inside her. "Where's Amberly?"

"You'll see her soon enough." Brian nodded to someone behind him, and the guard gripped her arm again. "Take her to her room and get her ready. Our guests will be arriving via yacht in a few hours, and I don't want to keep them waiting."

MONROE'S MIND raced through everything he needed to do as the copter zoomed through the air.

Ghost had arrived to pick them up.

First, the team had Ainsley stage a vehicle breakdown about a mile away. Their plan had worked, and the officer had been called to help.

That had presented them with a brief window of opportunity to leave the ranch. Monroe feared if the officer saw them leave that he'd call Brian—or someone connected with Brian—and give him a heads up.

At least, their guests were safe at the House of Winslow. That made Monroe feel a little better.

Hudson oversaw their tactical plan, which they'd been reviewing during the flight.

He'd brought Jesse, Sienna, Hayes, Ruger, and Mateo.

Mateo would be a big help since he'd been a Mexican federales. He still had a lot of contacts in the country.

At the last minute, he'd asked a man named Peyton Steel also to come. Peyton didn't work at Vanishing Ranch—not yet. Charlie had been trying to recruit him. But he was former CIA and brilliant. He had many of the skills that could be valuable for them on this mission.

Plus, Monroe needed to bring someone Brian wouldn't recognize—just in case the man had done his homework about their employees, which Monroe suspected he had.

Monroe glanced at his watch. They should be landing within the next hour.

Once on the ground, they'd need a plan so they could arrive at the island virtually unseen.

There were still a lot of things that needed to fall into place.

Failure wasn't an option.

———

As Charlie was led down the hallway, she glanced around.

Some of the doors around her were open.

She'd counted at least six other women here.

Women with hollow eyes and robotic movements.

Most likely, they'd been drugged.

Probably heroin.

Charlie was surprised she hadn't been injected with anything yet. The drugs would take away her drive to escape. Would make her more easily compliant.

But Brian no doubt had a plan.

He always did.

More disgust churned inside her.

All she could think about was Amberly. She didn't want her daughter to go through this. She wanted to protect her.

She only prayed her plan worked.

Not long ago, she'd met with Finley Cooper, the CEO of a company on the verge of some innovative technologies. Her company had developed a GPS tracker that could be swallowed like a pill.

The device would remain in a person's system for up to seventy-two hours before becoming inactive.

The problem was that it was still a prototype. Nothing had been approved. It might not be completely safe even.

But Charlie had purchased a few of the preliminary pills.

She was going to be the test subject to see if they worked.

The man escorting her opened a door at the end of the hallway and shoved her inside.

Charlie's heart raced as she anticipated what she might find in the room.

Then she saw the figure standing there and nearly turned to a puddle.

Amberly.

Amberly was in this room.

But was she okay?

CHAPTER
FORTY-NINE

MONROE and the gang arrived at the Mexican marina, and Hudson went to find a boat they could rent.

The weather was holding out.

But they still had some challenges.

He couldn't stand the thought of Charlie and Amberly suffering right now.

As Hudson talked to someone, Monroe wandered down the dock.

There were all kinds of boats here—from small fishing boats to huge yachts. It appeared one of the bigger boats—Ocean's Dream—was about to launch. Several dockhands were around it, and three men lingered on the deck.

Monroe watched it a moment.

"Wouldn't you like to have that kind of money?" A man paused beside him and stared at the boat.

He glanced at the guy—he appeared to work here. He spoke broken English, and he must have identified Monroe as an American because he didn't bother to speak Spanish.

"Yeah, I guess I would," Monroe asked. "Just some guys out taking a cruise?"

"Or something like that."

He did a double take at the man. "What do you mean?"

The guy shrugged. "Whenever a boat full of rich men stop this way, I know they're only headed to one place."

At once, reality hit Monroe.

He knew exactly what these guys were going to do.

And he'd just found his opening.

———

Charlie rushed to Amberly and pulled her into her arms. "Are you okay?"

"I'm so scared," Amberly said into her chest.

"I know, baby girl. It's okay to be scared sometimes."

That's when Charlie realized that Amberly hadn't pulled away.

This wasn't the way she'd wanted them to bond. Not at all.

Amberly stepped back and wiped her eyes with her sleeve.

"Is what that man said true? He's my father?" Her eyes were a well of confusion, terror, and a touch of hope that this was all a lie.

Brian had threatened to tell Amberly in front of her. Apparently, he hadn't been able to wait.

Charlie swallowed hard before nodding. "I'm sorry. It is."

A tear dripped down her cheek. "Who is he?"

"He married my mother after my dad died."

"So you had an affair with your stepfather?"

Charlie shook her head, unsure the correct way to share the truth. "No, sweetie. He . . . he attacked me."

"So I'm a product of . . ." Her voice trembled, but she didn't finish the statement.

Charlie didn't answer. Instead, she pulled Amberly into her arms again.

Tears rolled down her cheeks.

"I feel . . . dirty," she murmured.

"You have no reason to feel dirty."

"But . . ." She wiped her eyes.

"Sometimes the most beautiful things are born out of the hardest of circumstances."

Amberly stared at her. "You really believe that?"

"I do."

Before they could talk any more, the door opened, and someone stepped inside.

MONROE RECONVENED WITH HIS GUYS.

Mateo had found two boats they could rent.

Good. They would need them for their plan to work.

"You see that yacht over there?" Monroe nodded toward it. "It's headed toward the island. We need to take charge of the vessel."

Mateo nodded. "Meanwhile, we'll take the boats to the other side of the property and breech it from that side."

"Exactly." Monroe nodded at Peyton. "You'll need to take the lead on the yacht. Brian and his guys will recognize us."

"You don't think he's vetted the guys who are coming?" Peyton asked. "If he's gotten away with this for this long, he's smart enough to research them."

"I agree. We'll need to see what we can do to fool him. At least, it will be a distraction."

Hudson glanced at the boat. "How many people are aboard?"

"Five," Monroe told him. "I watched it for several minutes and asked one of the dockhands."

"We can take them out," Jesse said.

Monroe nodded, having no doubt that they could. These guys onboard weren't warriors. They were most likely spoiled businessmen who thought they could get away with murder because of their social and financial statuses.

"Hudson, what's the best way to board the boat?"

He pulled everyone around as they developed their plan.

————

Under the watchful eye of a woman who'd been sent into their room, Charlie and Amberly showered, dressed, and did their hair and makeup. Charlie had been given specific instructions to cover her bruises.

She'd done her best.

After the woman gave her approval of their look, Brian stepped back into the room.

"Now we just have to wait for our guests to arrive," he crooned.

Charlie stared at the man, not bothering to hide her contempt. "You're not drugging us?"

"Not all men prefer that."

Disgust burned her throat.

"Some men prefer to subdue their women themselves." Brian turned around to leave. "I'll come to get you soon."

As soon as he'd closed and locked the door, Amberly turned to Charlie. The girl looked on the verge of a mental breakdown. Her eyes were glassy with tears, her shoulders slumped, her breathing shallow.

"Mom, what are we going to do?" Amberly rushed.

It was the first time Amberly had ever called Charlie that.

Charlie swallowed hard before saying, "We're going to get out of this."

"How?"

"We're just going to have to trust each other."

Amberly glanced behind her, and her eyes widened.

"What is it?" Charlie turned to see what had caught her attention.

"Look out the window. It's a boat."

Charlie's lungs tightened.

That was the yacht full of men coming to the island, wasn't it?

CHAPTER
FIFTY-ONE

"TAKE HER," Brian muttered.

Charlie's heart lodged in her throat. "No!"

The last thing she wanted was to be separated from Amberly.

Panic raced through her at the thought.

"Mom!" As a man took Amberly's arm and led her toward the door, Amberly reached for Charlie. "Mom!"

She started to lunge toward her, but Brian grabbed her arm and held her back.

Charlie jerked her elbow back, and it collided with Brian's face.

He let out a yelp and released his grip.

As he did, Charlie darted toward Amberly.

But when the guard holding Amberly raised his gun to her head, Charlie froze.

"I wouldn't do that." The man looked at her with a daring look in his eyes.

She swallowed hard as she stared at Amberly.

"I'll find you," Charlie told her. "Be strong."

"Mom . . ."

Charlie's heart felt as if it was breaking.

How could she protect Amberly if they weren't together?

She didn't know how.

But she would figure out a way, she decided.

Suddenly, someone's fingers gripped her hair, tangling with her locks and pulling them until she gasped with pain.

Her scalp burned as her hair ripped from it.

Brian.

"I don't know who you think you are," he growled.

Her hands fisted. She wanted to fight back. To give this guy what he deserved.

But not at Amberly's expense.

She glanced at her daughter again, just as the guard pulled her from the room and slammed the door.

Then Brian turned toward her, disgust dripping from his eyes. "I can't wait to put you in your place. But not now. I'll save that for later."

With one last dirty look, he left her in the room

and slammed the door.

She heard the click of a lock behind him.

The locks were on the outside of the doors.

Of course.

She drew in a shaky breath, trying to ignore the sting on her scalp.

Then she walked over to the balcony.

Maybe she could see something happening outside. She could gather more information. Figure out something.

She'd learned to rely on herself. And she needed a backup plan just in case her team couldn't find them.

———

This was going to work.

It had to.

Monroe stared from the back of the yacht.

They'd coerced the captain into taking them to the island—albeit at gunpoint.

Meanwhile, one of the men onboard had looked similar enough to Peyton. They'd switched clothes. Got all the pertinent information from the guy.

The rest of the men were tied up downstairs. They couldn't risk any of these guys selling them out before they arrived at the island.

Monroe knew there could be serious repercussions for what they'd done, but the risk was worth it.

He could see the island in the distance.

Mateo and Hudson had taken their boats to the other side of the landmass, along with Hayes and Sienna, just as they'd discussed. They would try to find Amberly and Charlie, while Monroe, Ruger, and Peyton created a distraction.

Mexican law enforcement along with the FBI had also been informed and would be here to help—but not yet.

The Vanishing Ranch team needed to handle this themselves first. There was no time to waste.

They were almost at the dock.

And that meant it was almost showtime.

He prayed everything went according to plan.

CHAPTER
FIFTY-TWO

CHARLIE PUSHED down her nerves as she watched the boat come closer and closer to the island.

She wasn't sure what the next few hours would hold.

But she knew it probably wouldn't be good.

Where was Monroe? Had the tracker worked?

Because if it hadn't, how would he ever find her out here? These guys were good at being secretive. They hadn't been located all this time, so why would they be discovered now?

The tracker had to work. It *had* to.

She pressed her eyes together and lifted a prayer.

Dear Lord, You know the number of hairs on my head, and You care about the sparrows in the air. I know You care about me and every detail of my life too. But it's not my protection I want to pray for. Please cast your shield of protection over Amberly and the other women here. Use me to help them. Give me strength and wisdom.

Charlie opened her eyes and continued to stare at the yacht.

She wondered where Amberly was.

Based on what she knew about the situation, they would all be led into the large living room so they could pretend like they were at a party together.

Even though it was hard to pretend it was a party when they were unwilling participants.

Charlie had some fighting instincts and skills.

But she knew Brian was here along with six other guards. And who knew how many men were on this boat?

There's no way she could take them all out without any type of weapon. Even with a weapon, it would still be a challenge.

But her eyes widened when she saw that the boat was coming directly toward the shore—traveling too fast.

She glanced below her at the patio where Brian waited, dressed in a suit, for his clients to arrive.

What was he thinking right now?

He began to pace, which seemed to indicate something was amiss.

The next instant, the boat collided with a rock and

rammed into the dock. The sounds of the metal scraping and wood splintering made her cringe.

Brian muttered something beneath his breath before speaking into his phone.

No doubt he was calling the guards to see what had happened.

But Charlie had a feeling she knew exactly what was going on.

She prayed that she was correct.

———

Monroe braced himself for the impact.

He heard the sounds of the hull cracking and ripping apart until finally the boat came to a halt.

Three men came running toward them, none of them Brian.

And now it was truly showtime.

Peyton started toward what had once been the dock.

"What were you guys thinking?" one of the guards called.

"I don't know what happened. I need to talk to my captain. It isn't very well lit out here so we must've hit bottom."

"You just ruined a very expensive pier, and you *will* be paying for that," the guard continued.

"Oh yeah? What about our yacht?" As Peyton and the man continued to argue, Monroe slipped from the back of the boat.

Peyton could hold these guys up for a while.

Meanwhile Mateo and the rest of the crew should be at the back of the island by now.

Before stepping off the boat he glanced at his cell phone to check.

He did have a message from Mateo.

Arrived. Breaching. What's your stat?

Quickly, Monroe typed back.

Three guards here. Distracted by crash. Must get to the house now.

Will do.

He carefully dropped himself into the warm water, and quietly swam away from the boat, parallel with the shore.

Once he was a safe distance away, he climbed from the water onto the beach and then darted to some brush in the distance.

So far, so good.

He pushed himself through the brush, going toward the house.

He paused as he saw someone in the distance.

Was that . . . Charlie?

She stood on one of the balconies, watching everything that was happening.

His heart rate slowed a moment. She was okay.

Now he just had to ensure that she remained that way.

He took note of the dress she wore—it was black and small and . . . revealing.

Disgust roiled inside him.

She wouldn't choose an outfit like that on her own. No, she'd been forced to wear that, forced to put on something for the sake of the "guests" coming to the island.

He pushed down his anger at the thought.

Instead, he glanced at the house again and saw a stairway twenty feet away from him.

If he could make it there, then maybe he could make it inside the house.

He pushed through some more plants, trying to remain low as he tried to reach the stairway.

But just as he emerged from the brush, he spotted someone holding a gun and aiming directly at him.

Delilah.

"I was hoping I might see you again," she muttered with a gleam in her eyes. "Because I don't like to leave jobs unfinished."

CHARLIE SUCKED in a breath when she saw a movement to her left. It was on the other side of the patio from where Brian paced so he probably had no idea what was going on.

But was that . . . Monroe?

Her heart rate quickened.

It was.

He was here.

But now a woman with a gun faced off with him.

She held her breath as she waited to see what would play out.

Monroe hadn't had a chance to grab his own gun when she appeared.

So now his hands were raised, and he was at the mercy of the woman.

The only good news was that Monroe was

standing close to her.

That could make it easier for him to take her out if necessary.

But Charlie needed to do something to help.

She stepped back into her room and looked around.

There wasn't anything obvious that could be used as a weapon, and she was sure that it had been planned that way.

But there had to be something.

Her gaze finally stopped on a hairbrush that had been left in the bathroom.

She grabbed it and ran back out to the balcony.

She gripped it in her hands, wishing she could hear the conversation below.

But she couldn't.

She only knew that any second, this woman could pull the trigger and Monroe would be dead.

Charlie raised her arm and took aim.

———

"You don't want to do this." Monroe kept his hands in the air.

At the right opportunity, he was going to take the gun from her. He just needed to ensure she didn't pull the trigger first.

"I have a good track record of completing whatever I start. I don't plan on messing that up now."

"So you're going to shoot me?" The good news was that she hadn't picked up her phone to let anybody know he was here.

That could work to their advantage.

He felt his phone buzz in his pocket and knew it was probably Mateo with an update. Thankfully, the device had a waterproof case.

He hoped the rest of them were having better luck than he was.

At least Delilah didn't seem to notice the buzzing.

"I'm just trying to decide if I should make this quick and painless or if I want to draw it out and make it a little more fun," Delilah said with a sick grin.

Monroe just stared at her. "You don't have to do this at all."

"Sure, I do." She raised her gun again. "My reputation is on the line. On second thought, I should just get this over with."

As she said the words, something rustled the bushes beside them.

The distraction offered him just enough time to grab her gun and twist it from her hand.

The Glock fell into the brush.

Then the real struggle began.

CHARLIE FELT relief wash through her.

Her distraction had worked.

She watched as Monroe struggled with the woman.

Finally, he put her in a headlock.

A moment later, she sank to the ground.

She wasn't dead, but she would be unconscious for a while.

Charlie had to admit that she was impressed. She'd never seen Monroe use that skill before.

In the meantime, Monroe grabbed the woman's gun from the brush and tucked it into his waistband.

Then he looked up at Charlie.

Good. He'd seen her.

The nod he gave her seemed to indicate that he was on his way to help.

What should she do right now? Wait for him? Look for Amberly? Where was she even being held?

As the questions raced through her mind, she heard gunfire in the distance.

Three shots.

They'd all come from the direction of the yacht.

She wasn't sure exactly what had happened, but she imagined that Monroe had somebody stationed aboard it.

Somebody who had just taken out the guards that had gone to check things out.

Her gaze went back to Brian.

Her breath caught.

He was gone.

But where? He'd just been right there.

She scanned everything around her, but still didn't see him.

He must have gone back in the house.

If the guards who'd left to check out the boat had been taken out as well as Delilah, that still left two more that she knew about.

That was assuming the gunfire hit the guards and not some of her Vanishing Ranch operatives.

Her heart panged at the thought.

She prayed that wasn't the case.

Quickly, she turned from the balcony and headed inside.

There were simply too many unknowns.

She had to figure out a way to get out of this room and find Amberly before anything else happened.

———

Monroe paused to check his phone before going into the house.

Mateo and his crew had taken out the guards they'd encountered.

They were now headed toward the house.

Peyton had also taken out the guards around the boat.

This was a good start. But things could still go south.

He knew better than to celebrate too early.

Brian hadn't been captured yet.

Monroe stepped into the house and ran up the stairway. He glanced down a long hallway.

He saw no one.

Carefully, he began creeping toward the room where he'd seen Charlie.

He reached the door—he was nearly certain it was the right room—and pushed it open.

An empty room stared back at him.

His stomach clenched.

Brian must have come and gotten Charlie.

Monroe left the room and hurried to the end of the hallway.

Sounds came from inside some of the rooms—the sounds of crying.

More women were here, weren't they?

He would help them as soon as he could.

But Charlie and Amberly were in the most danger now.

He exited the hallway onto a mezzanine balcony showcasing the first floor.

Three people stood below him.

Charlie with her hands raised.

And Brian—with a gun to Amberly's head.

CHARLIE STARED AT BRIAN. "You don't want to do this."

"Sure, I do." He glanced up and sneered. "I'm all about self-preservation. Or didn't you notice? My helicopter is on the way."

"Leave Amberly here. Take me."

"No, thanks. My odds are better with Amberly."

Amberly let out a soft cry, one that broke Charlie's heart.

"Don't do it," someone demanded from above.

She knew that voice.

Monroe.

Her heart lifted.

He was here.

"Put your gun down." Brian's cheeks reddened as he began to unravel.

Charlie never remembered seeing him like this. He was always so in control.

But things had taken a turn.

"How did you find her?" Brian fidgeted. "I covered all my bases. She didn't have anything on her. I made sure of that. No one followed us. So how?"

Monroe slowly paced down the stairs. "That's not important. The important thing is that you know you're out numbered. I have seven other guys closing in right now as well as the Mexican federal police. There's no way you're walking away.

"I'm not going down for this."

"I think you are." Monroe stopped on the first level but remained a safe distance away.

Good. Charlie didn't want Brian to get trigger happy in his desperation.

"You've always feared Charlie would take you down one day, haven't you?" Monroe stared at him. "You've always known she was your biggest threat—not because of what you did to her. But because she's strong enough to stand up against you."

"You don't know what you're talking about!" Brian's hands trembled. "I have more guys on their way here. You think you've won. You haven't."

Charlie held her breath as she anticipated whatever Brian was planning next.

Monroe stared at Brian.

The gun the man held to Amberly's head was the only thing that made Monroe nervous.

Brian was just crazy enough to pull the trigger.

But he had to know that if he did, he'd also be a dead man.

Mateo and Hayes stood on the upper balcony, guns raised.

Hudson and Sienna stood across from Monroe.

Peyton, Jesse, and Ruger had remained by the docks, just to make sure there were no surprises—and to direct the police when they showed up.

"Only weak men prey on women," Monroe muttered.

"I'm not weak." Brian's voice trembled. "I'm smart."

At once, something seemed to ignite inside Amberly.

"No, you're not. You only think you're smart." She jammed her elbow into his gut.

Brian reeled from the sudden movement.

As he did, Charlie grabbed Amberly and pulled her away.

The next instant, she swung her leg around and toward the gun in Brian's hand.

The gun went flying.

He stood speechless a moment.

But only a moment.

Because as the police flooded inside, Brian immediately started spewing lies, threats and even offered the officers bribes.

They paid him no mind as they subdued him and placed him in handcuffs.

It appeared this was over—really over.

AS SOON AS the police had handcuffed Brian, Charlie rushed to Amberly and threw her arms around her. The teen clung to Charlie as tears rolled down her face.

"That was very brave what you did," Charlie murmured in her ear.

She sniffled. "I thought we were both going to die. It wasn't until then that I realized how much I really have to keep living for."

Charlie held her closer. "I know we both had a rough start to this, but maybe we can move on together from here."

Amberly nodded. "I'd like that."

Charlie continued to hold her as everything unfolded around them. As arrests were made. As a joint taskforce of the FBI and federales began to search for evidence.

A moment later, a paramedic came to check out Amberly.

As they went to the couch to sit down, Charlie turned.

Monroe stood there.

Her heart welled with love.

She tucked herself into his arms. "Thank you."

"You know I'd move heaven and earth for you."

She nodded. "I know. I am sorry I pulled away. It's just that . . ."

"You don't have to explain."

As she looked up into his face, she realized just how much she really did love him.

No one but Amberly knew the personal turn their relationship had taken. They'd kept it under wraps.

But she didn't care anymore.

She reached up and pressed her lips to his in a long kiss.

Until applause interrupted them.

Charlie pulled away with a chuckle and glanced at the group around her.

"It's about time," Jesse said.

"We've been rooting for you two for a long time," Sienna added.

Charlie took Monroe's hand into hers and turned to glance around.

Her gaze met Hudson's. "Did you get the rest of the women free?"

He nodded. "They're being treated right now. There were six others here, and they're in pretty rough shape. Most of them have been repeatedly shot up with heroin."

"I'm glad that they can finally get the help they need. I can only imagine what kind of files might be hidden here. Brian had dirt on so many people. I'm sure he was keeping tabs on everyone who came and went from this place—most likely without their knowledge."

"Don't worry, the federal authorities will be thoroughly investigating this place," Mateo said.

She glanced up and saw a surprising face appear.

Peyton.

Peyton offered her a nod. "Glad I could help out."

"Does this mean you're onboard?"

"I was originally going to say no. But after this assignment, I have changed my mind. I think I might be a good fit here."

"Welcome aboard then."

"Were you aware that Charity Boothe was being held here?"

She shrugged, unfamiliar with the name. "I'm not sure who you're talking about."

"Charity was also a CIA agent. She went missing two years ago. Then authorities found her body burned to a crisp. Or at least they assumed it was hers. They had a funeral. I attended it. But it turns out she isn't dead."

"You found her here?"

He nodded firmly. "She was hardly recognizable. But yes, she was being kept here."

"That's awful," Charlie said.

"I think we can safely say that the world is a better place now that Brian and his whole operation have been shut down," Hayes added.

"Here, here!" Sienna said.

"Let's have a big celebration when we return to the ranch," Charlie said. "You guys have truly been Charlie's Angels, and I'll be forever grateful to you for everything you've done."

"You're the one who brought us together," Jesse said. "And we know you'd do everything in your power to help any one of us. We're grateful to you also, boss."

"Now . . . enough of this sappy stuff. Let's talk more about this celebration you mentioned. What do you have in mind?" Sienna raised an eyebrow.

Charlie grinned, and her gaze stopped on

Monroe. "How about we celebrate with . . . a wedding?"

Another round of applause circled around them.

Monroe stepped closer and pulled her toward him. "I like that idea."

Charlie's grin widened.

So did his.

———

Two days later, everyone arrived safely back to Vanishing Ranch.

Brian and his guys had been arrested.

His organization had been shut down.

Numerous arrests had been made.

The people Brian had hired were ruthless. But many of them had nothing to lose—no strong family ties or political affiliations. They were people who'd already messed up so they dedicated their lives to pursuing money. Apparently, Brian had paid well.

As Monroe had said, "People who have nothing to lose may seem like good ones to hire. But having nothing to lose also means they'll quickly snitch on anyone in order to save themselves."

And they had. They were singing like songbirds, as the saying went. Brian had nothing to leverage over them, so several were trying to cut deals.

The feds were talking to former President Radar, but from everything she had heard the man appeared to be a puppet.

He had been a senator when the bombing of the Overland Hotel had occurred. And his outspoken stance against what had happened was what had ultimately gotten him elected as president.

In return, he owed a lot of people a lot of favors. He'd pretty much been in the pockets of men who had been involved with Brian's organization.

And Charlie was nearly certain he'd eventually be arrested also, but she knew the fact he'd been president would slow the process down.

They'd also discovered that Angelo had indeed been blackmailed. His ex-wife and daughter had been found safe. They'd been in hiding after threats had been made against them.

Detective Vincent had also been blackmailed and was now suspended from his job. The ranch was no longer under investigation.

Suzy would stay with them at Vanishing Ranch until she recovered.

Margaret had pulled through after her cardiac event, and they were moving her back home in a few days.

One of the women found on the island did turn out to be Charity Boothe. She was still coming out of her drug-induced state, but Charlie was forever grateful she'd been rescued along with the rest of the women on the island.

Even though these criminals had been uncovered and stopped, Charlie knew that there were more out there. There was more work to be done.

But for today, she would count this as a victory.

She'd also gotten the update when she'd returned that Bentley Prescott was doing okay. He had been moved out of ICU into a step-down unit. Charlie had already talked to him—he'd called her and said he planned on pursuing these people with everything the law could throw at them. He'd also admitted that he'd told the senator that Charlie was coming to the party. Though Bentley had asked the senator to keep it under wraps, the man must have told someone who'd then planned the whole fentanyl fiasco.

For now, Charlie wanted to concentrate on this ranch, on the new lodge being built, on starting her new life with Monroe . . . and mostly on getting to know Amberly better.

She still had a lot to learn about being a mom. But after this, she was fairly certain she could handle it. And she knew if Monroe was by her side that she would have his support and guidance throughout the process.

She was ready for a new chapter in her life.

And she was going to start now.

She was pleased to know that Sarah Chamberlain—Ruger's girlfriend—would be starting at the ranch soon as well. She'd be Charlie's executive assistant.

As they stepped back into her house, she turned to Amberly. "As you may have heard, I'm going to plan a wedding."

Amberly nodded. "I heard."

"I was hoping that you might be able to help me with some details."

Her eyes brightened. "You would want me to do that?"

"As a matter of fact, I would."

She nodded quickly. "I'd love to. But what about Jonathan? Are you going to fire him?"

"I'm going to have a talk with him, but I hope to give him another chance. Because we all deserve a second chance. But I'm going to set some very firm boundaries in place for the two of you. I think he's a good guy, and I know you're a good girl. But boundaries are definitely needed in this situation."

Amberly nodded. "Thank you. I'd like to stay at the ranch. It's starting to grow on me. I'm hoping that maybe I can help with some of the kids who come through."

"I would like that. And I'll teach you more about horses. You seem to like them."

"I do."

"Then I'll teach you how to work with them. And you can help me with my rescues and—"

"What about Sammy? We never rescued him."

Charlie grinned. "I actually had a friend of mine look into that. I had contacted him before everything went down—I just never had a chance to tell you. But if you go to the stables now, you'll see that Sammy is there."

Amberly let out a squeal. "Can she be my horse?"

"You want your own horse?"

"I've always wanted my own horse."

Charlie grinned. "That's good to know. I think we could work something like that out."

"Thank you!" Amberly threw her arms around Charlie again.

Joy filled Charlie's heart.

Their relationship would take a lot of work, and she was certain that there were still going to be very hard days ahead.

But she felt hopeful that the best was yet to come.

Finally, she could put closure on her past and look forward to a future of helping many more women and children find their way to a new life.

EPILOGUE

CHARLIE READJUSTED the bouquet in her hands as she stood inside the mess hall.

Amberly and Sienna stood with her.

She had chosen a simple white gown that stopped at her ankles. Since the air had a slight chill to it, she'd found a white shrug made from fake fur that she pulled around her shoulders. No veil—veils felt too fancy.

It sounded weird, but somehow, Charlie sensed her mom and dad's presence with her. Even though her parents' relationship hadn't ended well, she knew that somewhere deep inside, her mother had loved her.

And she had no doubt her dad had loved her and wanted the best for her.

Finally, she could put what happened to her

grandmother and father behind her. Justice could be served. Evil men would pay for their selfish actions.

Charlie felt certain that marrying Monroe would not hold her back from her life's mission, it would only make her life's mission easier.

"You ready for this?" Sienna asked.

Charlie nodded. "Without a doubt."

Then she hooked her arm through Amberly's and Sienna opened the door.

She stepped outside only to be greeted by a glorious sunset.

Monroe had made a cross out of some wood he'd found at the ranch. The symbol of hope was illuminated by this smear of brilliant colors in the sky behind them.

Chairs had been pulled from the mess hall and arranged in rows.

Chef had prepared a feast for them after the ceremony.

All her staff and crew from Vanishing Ranch were there—even Natalie and Joshua from the lodge.

Several guests who were currently staying with them were also present.

But mostly what Charlie noticed was Monroe as he stood at the end of the aisle.

He'd donned a cowboy hat, something he rarely wore. And instead of a tux, he'd chosen jeans and a white shirt. It seemed more appropriate for him out here on the ranch.

Amberly walked her down the aisle, and Pastor Larry asked Amberly's permission for Charlie to marry Monroe.

Amberly agreed.

Then Amberly sat in the front row, and Charlie joined hands with Monroe. She didn't often doubt her decisions. She wasn't that type of person.

Right now, she knew with full confidence that this was exactly what she needed to do.

"Charlie Soldier, do you take this man to be your lawfully wedded husband? To have and to hold from this day forward?"

She grinned at Monroe. "I do."

"Monroe Davis, do you take this woman to be your wife? To have and to hold from this day forward?"

Monroe's grin seemed to match hers. "I do."

Pastor Larry went through the rest of the ceremony in a matter of minutes. The next thing she knew, he was saying, "I now pronounce you husband and wife."

The two stepped together and met for a long kiss that had everyone around them cheering.

Charlie knew this was a new beginning, not just for her but for Vanishing Ranch.

She would keep moving forward with her mission here. Soon, she'd open Legacy Lodge: The Loretta to house women who'd been trapped in human trafficking. Carter Winslow had agreed to let her use the nearby house he'd purchased for whatever purposes Vanishing Ranch needed it for.

Good things waited in the future.

Charlie was certain of it.

~~~

Thank you for reading *Desperate Rescue*. If you enjoyed this book, please consider leaving a review.

Stay tuned for Vanishing Ranch: Legacy Lodge.
~~~

USA TODAY BESTSELLING AUTHOR
CHRISTY BARRITT
Buried
LEGACY
VANISHING RANCH · LEGACY LODGE ONE

ABOUT THE AUTHOR

USA Today has called Christy Barritt's books "scary, funny, passionate, and quirky."

Christy writes both mystery and romantic suspense novels that are clean with underlying messages of faith. Her books have sold more than three million copies and have won the Daphne du Maurier Award for Excellence in Suspense and Mystery, have been twice nominated for the Romantic Times Reviewers' Choice Award, and have finaled for both a Carol Award and Foreword Magazine's Book of the Year.

She is married to her Prince Charming, a man who thinks she's hilarious—but only when she's not trying to be. Christy is a self-proclaimed klutz, an avid music lover who's known for spontaneously bursting into song, and a road trip aficionado.

When she's not working or spending time with her family, she enjoys singing, playing the guitar, and exploring small, unsuspecting towns where people have no idea how accident-prone she is.

Find Christy online at:

www.christybarritt.com

www.facebook.com/christybarritt

www.twitter.com/cbarritt

Sign up for Christy's newsletter to get information on all of her latest releases here: **www.christybarritt. com/newsletter-sign-up/**

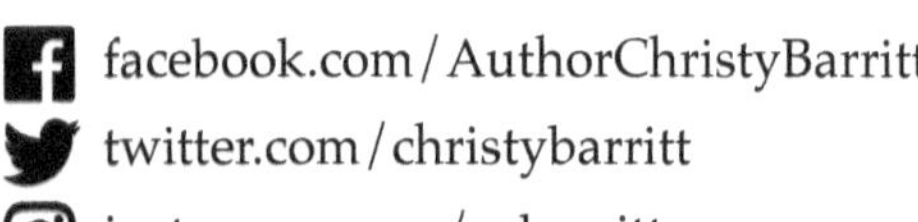

facebook.com / AuthorChristyBarritt

twitter.com / christybarritt

instagram.com / cebarritt

www.ingramcontent.com/pod-product-compliance
Lightning Source LLC
Chambersburg PA
CBHW031436160726
47994CB00005B/1754